THE ULTIMATE BRAAI MASTER

ROADS LESS TRAVELLED

JUSTIN BONELLO

 WITH BERTUS BASSON & MARTHINUS FERREIRA

WRITTEN BY HELENA LOMBARD

PENGUIN BOOKS

First published by Penguin Books (South Africa) (Pty) Ltd, 2013
A Penguin Random House company

Registered Offices: Block D, Rosebank Office Park, 181 Jan Smuts Avenue,
Parktown North, Johannesburg 2193, South Africa

www.penguinbooks.co.za

ISBN 978-0-14-353851-6

Written by Justin Bonello and Helena Lombard
Contributors: Bertus Basson, Marthinus Ferreira and the Ultimate Braai Master Teams
Recipe testing by Janet Gird
Photography by Louis Hiemstra and Dominique Little
Food styling by Caro Gardner
Design and layout by twoshoes.co.za
Cartography supplied by Chris Berens
Printed and bound by CTP Printers, Cape Town

CONTENTS

FOREWORD

When you're on the road with over 50 friends and crew members, filming a reality show for two months straight, travelling the length and breadth of South Africa and putting about 8000 km on your car's clock, a couple of things are bound to come bubbling up from beneath the surface.

From a traveller's point of view, it's that there are so many breathtaking places waiting to be explored in South Africa, places that even my well-travelled crew and I had never been to; that no matter how hardcore one back road might be, there's an even more challenging and beautiful one just around the next bend; and that even the smallest of small towns have a traffic cop hiding under the shade of one lonely tree waiting to catch you out. And you learn that just when you think there's no more space to fit anything into the boot of your car, you'll still be able to pack that kitchen sink after a well-thought-out reshuffle. It's like playing *Tetris*.

Then there's getting homesick, which inevitably happens when you're on the road for two months – no matter how spectacular your surroundings are. When homesickness strikes, it's good to know that you have loads of friends around to lift you up when you're feeling down (yes, like the song) because, let's face it, we're all human and we're bound to have our 'moments'. But there is a bonus for being away from home for so long: when you finally do arrive back at the doorstep of your house, you are treated like a long-lost war hero (score!).

And let's not forget about filming the show – the reason (and excuse) for us all to be there: it meant that we often worked 16-hour days and that we burnt a lot of energy. Writing this book while we were on the road was a great excuse to feed the starving masses some delicious braaied dishes along the way, on shoot days and every day in between. You'll spot the crew and contestants in most of the photos, and I would introduce them to you, but that would take forever. So you can name them and pretend that they're your friends and that you were there.

I also have to mention that, even though we were grafting hard for two months, we still found the time to light our own fires, get together and kuier. After all, that's what being South African is all about ...

Thank you to my loyal *Cooked* family and colleagues for an epic adventure and thanks to my readers for buying this book. Now get out there and create your own memories around the fire!

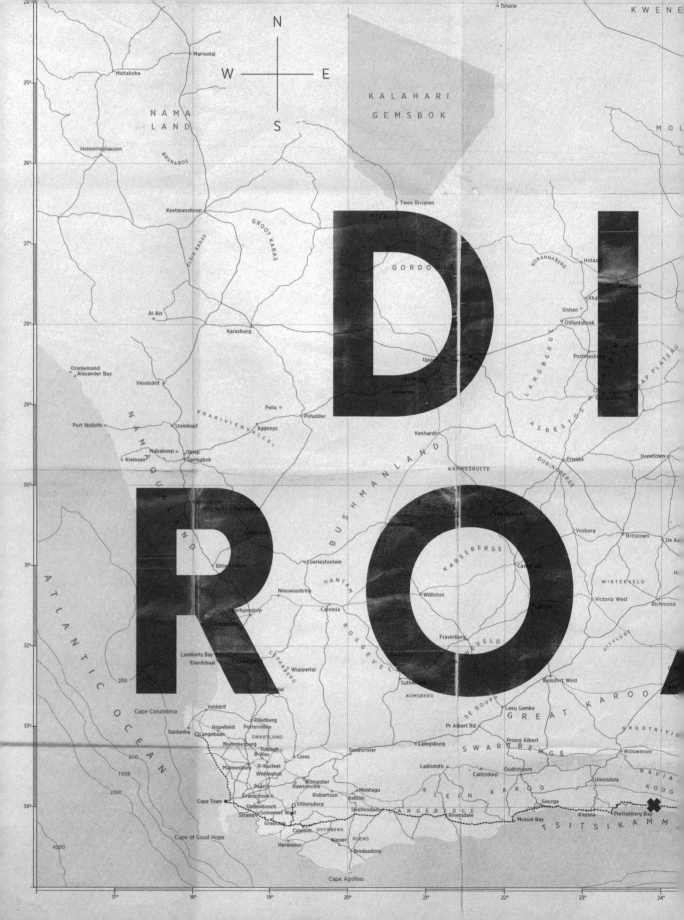

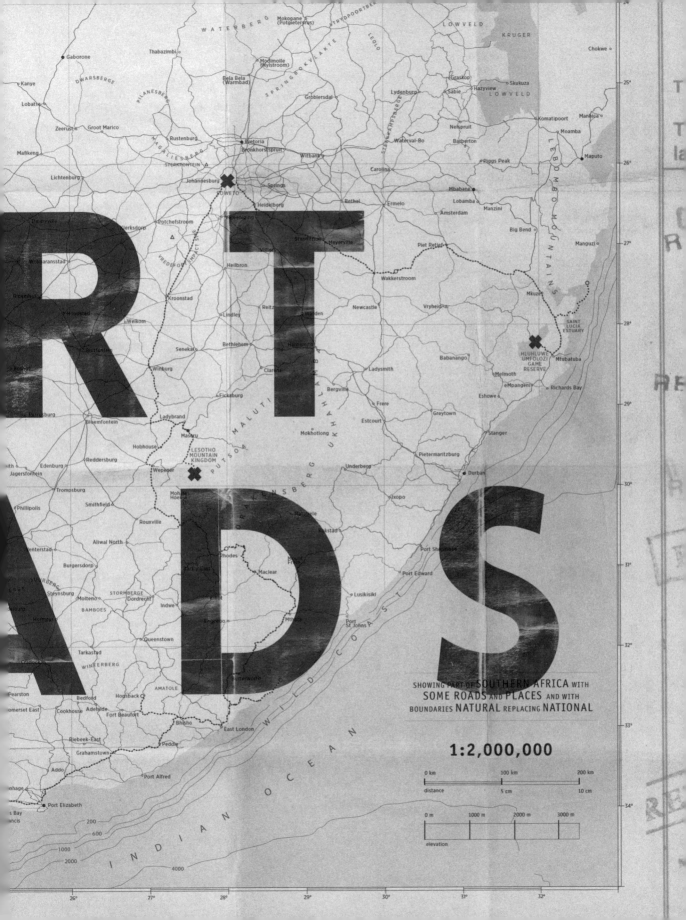

SHOWING PART OF SOUTHERN AFRICA WITH
SOME ROADS AND PLACES AND WITH
BOUNDARIES NATURAL REPLACING NATIONAL

1:2,000,000

| 0 km | | 100 km | | 200 km |
| distance | | 5 cm | | 10 cm |

| 0 m | 1000 m | 2000 m | 3000 m |
| elevation | | | |

HLUHLUWE

UMFOLOZI GAME RESERVE

★

Hluhluwe
SodwanaBay

↓ P453

HLUHLUWE UMFOLOZI GAME RESERVE

HLUHLUWE GAME RESERVE WAS MY FIRST STOP ON WHAT PROMISED TO BE AN EPIC 8000-KM ROAD TRIP INTO SOME OF THE MOST UNTOUCHED AND UNEXPLORED NOOKS AND CRANNIES OF SOUTH AFRICA.

AFTER TRAVELLING FOR ABOUT FOUR HOURS NORTH OF DURBS, I FOUND MYSELF IN ZULULAND, A SPOT WHERE, ONCE YOU ACTUALLY MANAGE TO GET OFF THE ROAD IN ONE PIECE, YOU CAN SIT BACK WITH A COLD BEER IN YOUR HAND AND BREATHE IN THE PANORAMIC VIEWS. IN THIS SPACE I ONCE AGAIN REALISED THE STARK CONTRAST BETWEEN PRESENT-DAY LIFE IN THE CITY AND HOW THINGS USED TO BE BEFORE THE HUMAN RACE ALL BUT DESTROYED OUR NATURAL RESOURCES. I SAT ON THE EDGE OF THE HILLTOP RESORT, OVERLOOKING THE GREEN, LUSH HILLS, AND JUST FOR A MOMENT I COULD IMAGINE WHAT LIFE USED TO BE LIKE BEFORE THE ARRIVAL OF THE ZULUS, THE VOORTREKKERS AND ALL THE NOISE AND DESTRUCTION OF LIFE AS WE KNOW IT TODAY. I WAS IN MY ELEMENT.

AND HOW DO YOU CELEBRATE BEING IN PARADISE WITH A VIEW THAT GOES ON FOREVER IN EVERY DIRECTION? THE WAY ANY HOT-BLOODED SOUTH AFRICAN WOULD. YOU LIGHT A FIRE AND PREPARE A FEAST FIT FOR A (ZULU) KING. AND ONCE THAT MEAT IS SIZZLING, ONCE THE DRINKS ARE FLOWING AND YOU ARE SURROUNDED BY THE COMFORTING NOISE OF FRIENDS AND FAMILY CHATTERING AWAY, YOU'LL KNOW, FOR THAT MOMENT, THAT EVERYTHING IS RIGHT WITH YOUR WORLD. AND **THIS** IS WHAT A BRAAI IS ALL ABOUT. **NOTHING** CAN BEAT IT.

AND LISTEN, IF THE TRAVEL BUG BITES, I URGE YOU TO START IN YOUR OWN BACKYARD. THIS COUNTRY IS A GEM, AND AS SOON AS YOU HIT THE BACK ROADS, YOU'LL REALISE JUST HOW LUCKY WE ARE TO LIVE HERE.

Way back when (sometime in the early 1800s), this area was the hunting ground of the Zulu Kingdom. And not long after that, the Great White Hunters arrived on their ox wagons. During this time (and in less than 50 years), hundreds of thousands of animals were hunted, leading to the extinction of many species.

Today it's refreshing to know that deep in the heart of rural Zululand, there is still a piece of paradise where animals can roam freely between the corridor of Hluhluwe and Umfolozi (a route which creates the perfect ecosystem, just the way nature intended). Originally, this area was made up out of three different reserves, but in 1989 they joined forces under one title. Through massive conservation efforts, Hluhluwe Game Reserve became responsible for the survival of one of South Africa's most endangered species: the rhino. In fact, when I drove in at the gates, it wasn't 2 km before I spotted my first rhino family. I hope future generations get to experience the same magic one day.

PUT YOUR GAME FACE ON!

- Pack some drinks – I'm talking about a fully packed cooler box filled with ice, G&T for the ladies, brandy and Cokes for the okes and of course, loads of lekker things to snack on.

- Make sure you've got a decent pair of binoculars. There's nothing worse than spotting an animal far away but not being able to see it properly. Kind of defeats the purpose.

- If you do spot an animal, sit still and keep quiet. Definitely not the optimal time to sneeze either.

- Put your phones and cameras on silent. Don't be THAT person.

- Don't wear a safari suit, stupid.

- Take a blanket if you're going out at night and a flask of coffee if you're going out early in the morning. You'll be so happy you did!

- Add some Amarula to that coffee.

- If it's an early morning game drive, be sure to eat breakfast before you go. You don't want to scare any animals away with the sound of your stomach eating itself.

- Take some biltong. For you, NOT a lion.

- If you're a bird lover (of the feathery, flying kind) – aka twitcher in the making – take a bird book with you. You never know what you might spot ... which is kind of the point.

- Wee before you go – especially if you're a girl.

- No matter how desperate you are (because you stupidly forgot the above), you can't get out of the vehicle. EVER.

SOUP IS THE UNIVERSAL LANGUAGE OF WINTER COMFORT FOOD, AND JUST BECAUSE YOU'RE SOMEWHERE IN THE MIDDLE OF NOWHERE, FREEZING YOUR BUTT OFF IN THE COLD, DOESN'T MEAN YOU CAN'T PULL THIS OFF ON YOUR BRAAI IN LESS THAN TWO HOURS. IT'S A HEARTY SOUP THAT CAN BE ENJOYED AROUND A CRACKLING FIRE. THE COMBINATION OF SOUP AND FIRE WILL WARM YOU UP AND LEAVE YOU FEELING *JUUUUST* RIGHT.

WHITE BEAN AND SMOKED FETA SOUP

 MARTHINUS FERREIRA

THIS RECIPE MAKES ENOUGH FOR FOUR PEOPLE.

★ THE SOUP

YOU'LL NEED:

200 g butter

2 onions, roughly chopped

3 garlic cloves, chopped

a small handful of fresh thyme

500 g dried white kidney beans, soaked in water overnight

a small jug of water, enough to cover the beans

1 litre of milk

salt and cracked black pepper, to taste

First up, get your fire ready and once the coals are medium to hot, put a fire-friendly pot on top of the grid. Add a chunk of butter, then once it has melted, stir in the chopped onions and garlic. As soon as the onions are soft, add a handful of fresh thyme sprigs and the white kidney beans. Cover with water and pour in about a litre of milk. Control the heat of the coals, so that the beans simmer (not boil – think 'potjie pot whisper') and let the soup cook for about one and a half hours, or until the beans are soft. At this point, you can choose to leave the soup chunky, which means you just have to remove the thyme, or smooth, pouring the slightly cooled beans into a blender and blitzing the soup until it resembles a purée. Season with salt and cracked black pepper and add a splash of milk to the soup if it's too thick for your taste.

⭐ THE SMOKED FETA

YOU'LL NEED:

150 g block of Danish feta

a couple of handfuls of oak chips pre-soaked in water for at least 30 minutes, for smoking

a roasting tin, with a wire rack that fits inside

a kettle braai (or anything similar with a lid and air vents)

Most people are terrified of smoking food, let alone cheese, but it's actually really simple and quick to do. You can smoke the feta just before the soup is ready. As soon as you have coals that are moderate to cool, scrape them to the sides of the braai and gooi a couple of handfuls of soaked oak chips straight onto the coals. Put the whole block of Danish feta (that's the melt-in-your-mouth smooth kind) onto the wire rack inside the roasting tin, pop it onto the centre of the braai grid and stick the lid onto the braai (with the air vents slightly open). Because the feta is on top of the wire rack, it's not in contact with any direct heat, so it shouldn't melt, but keep a close eye on it just in case. Smoke the feta for about five minutes or until it's turned a yellowish brown colour.

⭐ THE CROUTONS

YOU'LL NEED:

a couple of slices of white bread, cut into cubes

olive oil

Making croutons is dead simple. Make them in advance, on the same fire that your soup is simmering on. Heat a glug of olive oil in a pan, whack in about two handfuls of cubed bread and fry until the bread is gold and crispy. Drain on a kitchen towel. The alternative is simply to brush a couple of slices of white bread with olive oil, place them on the grid and toast them until gold and crispy on both sides. Once cooled down, cut the toast into crouton-sized cubes.

⭐ LADLE UP!

Grab four soup bowls and ladle in the soup. Top it off with a squeeze of lemon juice, crumbled up smoked feta and crunchy croutons, and slurp the cold away.

APPLE AND SAGE PORK SAUSAGES WITH SWEET MUSTARD SAUCE

 BY BERTUS BASSON

OTHER THAN BERTUS'S LOVE AFFAIR WITH HIS GIRLFRIEND MARELI, HIS DOG PATAT AND HIS AWARD-WINNING STELLENBOSCH RESTAURANT OVERTURE, HE ALSO HAS A SKELMPIE ON THE SIDE CALLED DIE WORSROL: A TRAVELLING CARAVAN THAT SERVES UP SOME OF THE BEST HOTDOGS IN THE COUNTRY. SO FOR YOU TO GET YOUR HANDS ON A BERTUS BASSON SAUSAGE RECIPE IS FIRST PRIZE. SERVE THE PORK SAUSAGE WITH BREAD, POTATO SALAD OR WHATEVER TICKLES YOUR FANCY, BUT ALWAYS HAVE A JAR OF SWEET MUSTARD SAUCE ON THE TABLE. LIKE BERTUS SAYS: 'IT JUST WORKS.'

LUCKILY FOR YOU, BERTUS GETS THAT NOT EVERYONE IS GOING TO GO OUT AND MAKE THE SAUSAGE MEAT FROM SCRATCH, SO THE RECIPE HE GAVE ME USES READY-MINCED PORK (AVAILABLE AT MOST BUTCHERS). IF YOU WANT TO KNOW HOW TO MAKE THIS MINCE, WATCH EPISODE 1 OF *ULTIMATE BRAAI MASTER II*, OR GO VISIT BERTUS AT HIS RESTAURANT AND BRIBE HIM WITH A BOTTLE OF GOOD WHISKEY. HE'S A KEEN TEACHER AND IF YOU'RE LUCKY, YOU MIGHT JUST CATCH HIM IN ACTION.

You can prep all of this in your kitchen at home, but you *have* to braai the sausages to get that umami taste!

YOU'LL NEED:

150 ml olive oil

2 onions, peeled and finely chopped

2 garlic cloves, sliced

1 teaspoon of cayenne pepper

1 teaspoon of allspice

2 tablespoons of paprika

a decent pinch of salt and black pepper

4 apples, cored and diced (skins still on)

1 kg pork mince, with no more than 10% fat

a handful of celery leaves, chopped

a big handful of sage, chopped

200 g finely cubed pancetta

about 100 g sausage casings (30 mm diameter), cleaned by running water through them, and soaked in fresh water overnight to make them easy to use

★ PORK SAUSAGES

Splash some olive oil into a pan then add the finely chopped onions, all the garlic and spices (except the celery leaves and sage) and sweat until tender. Remove from the heat and let it cool down completely. Next, put the chopped apples in a pan with a bit of oil and let them slowly caramelise. There's no need to add sugar – the apples are naturally sweet. Once they've got a bit of colour, take them off the heat and let them cool down.

Mix all the ingredients with the pork mince, including the finely cubed pancetta, celery leaves and the chopped sage, then work the meat for at least five minutes by kneading it like you would bread dough. By working the meat, you allow the protein to stretch and that's a good thing. To understand this, compare the difference between boerewors and German sausage. You don't want to overwork the meat that you put into boerewors, because it still needs to come apart slightly when you bite into it. When you really work and stretch the protein it makes it bind together better, like you would expect in a good pork sausage.

Now for the only tricky part: getting the mince into the sausage casings. If you have a handy electronic mincer, this should be easier. If you don't, use a hand-driven one (it works just as well). Make sure the casings are clean and moist. Slide the casing up onto the sausage funnel of the mincer (yep, pretty much like you would roll on a condom). Hold on to the casing end with your one hand (pinching it closed with your thumb and forefinger) and then slowly push the mince through the top. Once the meat starts going into the casing, let the filled casing slide over your hand naturally ... like a snake. Once the casing is filled, tie a knot at both ends. Keep stuffing sausage casings until you've used up all the mince.

★ TIPS FROM BERTUS

- The fat content in any type of sausage should never be more than 10%.
- Mincing works better if the meat stays cold. If it gets too warm, it won't go through the mincer, as warm fat becomes sticky.
- Always cook a small batch of the mince first before putting it in the casings. Taste it and adjust the flavour if it's not to your liking.
- Don't stuff the sausage too tightly or it will explode when you braai it.

★ SWEET MUSTARD

YOU'LL NEED:
6 egg yolks
3 tablespoons of mustard powder
100 g sugar
150 ml spirit vinegar

In a pot over a medium heat, whisk all the ingredients vigorously so that the eggs don't scramble. The mustard is done once it's heated through. Pour the mustard into a sealable jar. It will keep in your fridge for weeks, but then again it's so good, it might not.

IF YOU BOUGHT LAST YEAR'S BRAAI BOOK, YOU'VE PROBABLY TRIED THE RECIPE FOR BERTUS'S MOM'S APPLE PIE. THIS SIMPLE YET DELICIOUS PIE WAS ONE OF THE MOST POPULAR DISHES IN THE BOOK. IN FACT, I MADE IT WHILE ON A TRIP TO THE KAROO WITH MY CREW. THREE TIMES. THIS YEAR, BERTUS GAVE US ANOTHER PIE RECIPE – THIS TIME SAVOURY, NOT SWEET, BUT *DEFINITELY* THE STUFF OF LEGENDS. BE WARNED THOUGH … ONCE YOU TASTE IT, A NORMAL POTATO BAKE WILL NEVER, EVER BE THE SAME AGAIN!

P O T A T O   P I E

BY BERTUS BASSON

First up, pour the milk into a pot and once boiling, add the sliced potatoes, the garlic and a pinch of both nutmeg and cayenne pepper. Season with salt and pepper to taste. Bring the mixture down to a simmer, and stir continuously until it thickens and the potatoes are cooked but not mushy. (A word of warning: if the potato slices are too thick, they won't cook in the milk.)

Pop the potatoes into a baking dish – Bertus used a deep enamel plate, but you can use any round baking dish you can get your hands on. If you're baking it in the oven, feel free to use a glass dish, but if you're fire-baking it, use a non-stick baking tin. Pour most of the cream over the potatoes, followed by a handful of grated Parmesan – enough to cover the dish – and a generous dollop of crème fraîche. Put the baking dish of potatoes to the side and allow to cool while you whisk together the leftover cream (about 50 ml), one egg and a pinch of sugar.

YOU'LL NEED:

750 ml milk

about 4 large potatoes, peeled and very thinly sliced

2 garlic cloves, crushed

a pinch of nutmeg

a pinch of cayenne pepper

salt and pepper, to taste

about 2 cups of cream

a handful of Parmesan, grated

about 2 heaped tablespoons of crème fraîche

1 egg, whisked

a pinch of sugar

1 roll of puff pastry

a baking tin

SERVE WITH A Sunday braai, SPRINGBOK FILLET (page 19) or by itself with a salad. *So lekker!*

Take the puff pastry and place it on top of the floured surface. Using a rolling pin (or empty wine bottle) roll out the pastry and brush the top with some of the egg and cream mixture (keeping a bit aside). Carefully lift the pastry and place it over the potato bake, brushed side at the bottom. Cut off any excess dough hanging over the side of the glass dish or baking tin, then secure the dough over the potato bake by pressing it down with your hands at both the top and the bottom. The idea is to seal the pie completely so that no air will escape and the pastry will puff up. If you're feeling creative, you can take the pastry off-cuts and make leaves, roses, shapes or your girlfriend's / boyfriend's name. If you have two left hands (or no thumbs), don't worry … a couple of leaves won't change the taste of the dish, but it does look mightily impressive if you do get it right.

The last step is to brush the top of the pie with the remaining egg and cream mixture. Because of the sugar, the pie topping will caramelise and bake to a perfect golden brown.

If you're making the pie in the kitchen (sissy!), bake for about 30 to 45 minutes at 180 °C, or until golden brown. If you're doing it on the fire, hang a flat-bottomed potjie over medium to hot coals and place the baking dish inside. Pop the lid on, put a scattering of coals on top and bake until ready (golden brown). You can also bake this inside a kassie – definitely a skill worth learning (page 124).

SPRINGBOK IS NOTORIOUSLY DIFFICULT TO COOK IN AN OVEN, LET ALONE ON A FIRE. THIS IS TRUE FOR MOST TYPES OF GAME MEAT, BECAUSE OF THE LOW FAT CONTENT. HERE'S A FAIL-PROOF WAY TO BRAAI A SPRINGBOK FILLET PERFECTLY, EVERY TIME.

HERB-CRUSTED RUBBED SPRINGBOK

 MARTHINUS FERREIRA

★ THE SPRINGBOK FILLET

Crush the garlic, strip the thyme leaves off the sprigs and mix well with all the spices.

Put the fillet in a big bowl and rub the spices thoroughly into the meat – pretend you're massaging a pretty girl with loads of knots in her shoulders ... in other words: really get in there. Make sure the fillet is completely covered in spices and let it rest for at least an hour ... longer if you can. The general rule of thumb is that the bigger the piece of meat, the longer it'll need to rest in the rub, and the more rub you'll need.

As soon as the coals are ready (moderate to hot) braai the fillet for about four to five minutes a side. Any more than this and it will lose all those lekker natural flavours. Let the meat rest for about five minutes before slicing.

YOU'LL NEED:

2 garlic cloves, crushed

4 or 5 sprigs of fresh thyme

200 g coarse sea salt

50 g ground coriander

40 g white sugar

5 g paprika

a springbok fillet

★ CHARRED BROCCOLI & ASPARAGUS

This is one of the easiest veg side dishes you can do on a braai, and it's packed with flavour. Make sure you don't overcook the vegetables – they still have to go 'crunch' when you bite into them.

First off, break the back ends off the asparagus (where it would naturally break if you had to bend it) and only use the spears. Put the asparagus into rapidly boiling salted water for a minute, then take it out and plonk it into iced water (fancy word for this is blanching). Do the same with the broccoli, but boil for three minutes before putting it into the iced water. Next, make the dressing, mixing together the olive oil, garlic, chilli and salt and pepper. Toss the vegetables in the dressing, then arrange the broccoli and asparagus inside a sandwich grid. Place over a hot fire and braai until charred – about two to three minutes a side. Put the vegetables back into the dressing bowl and toss one more time.

YOU'LL NEED:

a big handful of asparagus

2 big handfuls of broccoli stems

200 ml olive oil

garlic and chilli, to taste, finely chopped up

salt and black pepper, to taste

 SERVE WITH The springbok fillet and POTATO PIE (page 16). Easy and tasty!

RULE THE ROOST

THERE ARE SOME PRETTY NIFTY SKILLS YOU CAN LEARN IF YOU'RE EVER FACE-TO-FACE WITH A WHOLE CHICKEN AND YOU WANT TO DO SOMETHING DIFFERENT WITH IT ON THE BRAAI, OTHER THAN STICKING A BEER CAN UP ITS ... (AND THEN HOPING IT COOKS THROUGH IN TIME FOR LUNCH). ALL YOU NEED IS A SMALL SHARP KNIFE, A MEDICAL KIT ON HAND (IF YOU'RE AN ACCIDENT-PRONE NOVICE), A PROPER BUTCHER'S BLOCK (ONE THAT WON'T SLIP AROUND – SEE NOTE ON ACCIDENT-PRONE NOVICE), A LITTLE PATIENCE AND, OF COURSE, A CHICKEN. BERTUS AND MARTHINUS ARE PROS WHEN IT COMES TO BIRDS, SO I LET THEM SHOW ME HOW TO DO THIS. AND YES, THE KID IN ME TIMED THEM.

SPATCHCOCKING

BY BERTUS BASSON

IN THE WINK OF AN EYE

1 Put the chicken on its back, with its legs towards you.

2 Cut through the backbone and rib bones.

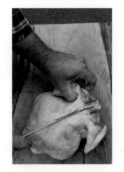

3 Pull the chicken open.

4 Remove all excess skin on the inside.

5 Turn the chicken over and pat yourself on the back.

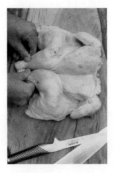

YOU'RE DONE!

GO TO PAGE 26 FOR THE PERI-PERI SPATCHCOCK RECIPE.

JOINTING

BY MARTHINUS FERREIRA

LESS THAN *3* MINUTES

1 Put the chicken on its back, tail towards you.

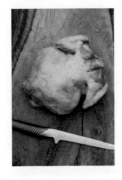

2 Cut the wishbone out.

 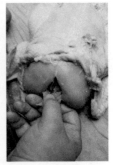

3 Turn the chicken onto its front and break its backbone by pulling the drumsticks towards each other.

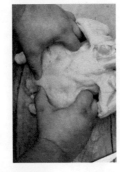

4 Cut the leg away from the backbone and repeat this on the other side. You can choose to divide each leg into a drumstick and a thigh, but I think the thigh is the best part of any leg.

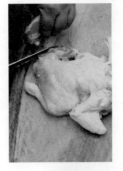

5 Snap the wing to one side and cut it off. Repeat on the other side.

6 Cut down the middle of the chicken, slowly removing the breast by cutting it off the carcass. Do this on both sides and keep the cartilage and carcass for chicken stock.

YOU'RE DONE!

GO TO PAGE 30 FOR THE ORIENTAL CHICKEN RECIPE.

DEBONING

BY BERTUS BASSON

LESS THAN 5 MINUTES

1 Put the chicken on its back, tail towards you. Cut the skin open down the centre – lengthways from neck to tail.

2 Starting at the neck, loosen the skin all the way around the carcass on both sides.

3 Cut through the thigh bone that is attached to the back of the carcass and loosen it on both sides. Once done, your chicken should now look something like this.

4 At the neck, cut through the wing bone to loosen the breast.

5 Loosen the flesh off the bone and cut the carcass loose from the breast, using small quick nicks.

Your chicken hopefully now looks like this. Next cut the carcass loose from the other side.

6 Cut along the bottom of the cartilage to get the carcass out. Use this for making chicken stock.

7 Locate the wishbone and remove it by cutting and pulling it out. (Yes, okay. Find a friend and make a wish.)

Remove all the extra cartilage still stuck on the meat.

8 Pull the legs to the bottom (skin side down) and make an incision through one, and then the other, to reveal the bone inside each.

Snap each leg. Pull out the drumstick bone and cut it off. Repeat on the other side. Trim off the cartilage that stayed behind on both sides.

9 Remove most of the wing by cutting out the main bone (that's the bigger bone of the wing).

10 Loosen the skin on the sides by gently pulling it off the flesh.

11 Fold in the flesh to where the carcass used to be (on both sides).

Fold the skin over the flesh to wrap it up.

HAVE A BEER. YOU DESERVE IT.

GO TO PAGE 28 FOR THE TANDOORI CHICKEN ROLL RECIPE.

WHAT IS IT WITH SOME PEOPLE TODAY – COMPARING CHICKENS TO VEGETABLES? IT'S THE MOST BIZARRE THING – ESPECIALLY IF YOU THINK ABOUT THE FACT THAT CHICKEN USED TO BE MADE FOR A SUNDAY LUNCH AS A SPECIAL TREAT. TODAY OUR MEAT CONSUMPTION HAS BECOME SO BAD THAT WE NO LONGER SEE A PIECE OF CHICKEN AS SOMETHING DELICIOUS, BUT RATHER AS A SIDE DISH OR SOMETHING TO EAT AT THE END OF THE MONTH. LET ME TELL YOU, THERE ARE FEW THINGS IN LIFE AS SIMPLE AND DELICIOUS AS A GOOD OLD-FASHIONED CHICKEN BRAAI. IT'S EASY TO DO ONCE YOU KNOW THE BASIC TRICKS, AND IT WON'T COST YOU AN ARM AND A LEG (OR A THIGH) TO MAKE. WHILE MY CREW AND I WERE FILMING IN HLUHLUWE, WE HAD A DAY OFF, AND THAT INEVITABLY MEANT TWO THINGS. ONE, WE PARTIED LATE INTO THE NIGHT, AND TWO, THERE WERE A LOT OF RED-EYED, RAVENOUS CREW MEMBERS IN NEED OF A SECOND LUNCH THE MORNING AFTER. SO THIS WAS THE PERFECT DAY TO REVIVE THE CHICKEN ON THE BRAAI (AND TO REVIVE MY BLURRY-EYED CREW).

A GOOD OLD-FASHIONED
CHICKEN BRAAI

 JUSTIN BONELLO

Here are three ways to do a chicken braai. My personal favourite is the peri-peri spatchcock – hot enough to wake any zombie from their worst hangover – and a great excuse to have cold beers on the table.

For those of you who don't know how to spatchcock a chicken, cut it into braai pieces or debone it, go to page 20 before trying these recipes. Then invite some friends and family over, light fires, play good tunes and just celebrate the simple side of life, one chicken at a time.

RULES OF A CHICKEN BRAAI

★ I won't eat anything other than a free-range or organic bird. Those commercially produced ones are not my style. And real food just tastes so much better.

★ Sealing the bird is important, so do that first.

★ Braai on moderate coals so that the skin doesn't burn.

★ Don't overcook it – 45 minutes per kg, brushing with the leftover marinade as you go.

★ If you stab the thickest part of the chicken and the juices run clear, it's ready to eat.

★ PERI-PERI SPATCHCOCK

This is probably the simplest of the chicken recipes, and definitely my favourite – probably something to do with my Portuguese heritage. The peri-peri sauce is ten chillies strong, so if you can't handle the heat, don't try this ... unless you add less chilli, but that kind of defeats the purpose. For the rest of you, go ahead. It'll become a family favourite in no time. *Fast food chicken se moer!*

For the peri-peri sauce recipe, go to page 111 and to figure out how to spatchcock a (free-range) chicken check out page 21. Once you've done that, let the chicken sleep in the marinade overnight – in the fridge.

Braai on a moderate fire, bone side first and baste with the leftover marinade as you go, turning the chicken over about every ten minutes.

 SOUTHERN-STYLE SLAW (page 34), fresh bread rolls and icy cold beer for the burn.

THIS IS THE MOST DIFFICULT OF THE THREE CHICKEN RECIPES BECAUSE YOU HAVE TO DEBONE A WHOLE CHICKEN. CHECK OUT PAGE 25 TO SEE HOW TO DO THAT. IF YOU CAN'T BE BOTHERED TO DEBONE, JOINT OR SPATCHCOCK THE CHICKEN, STUFF THE CORIANDER UNDERNEATH THE SKIN AND DO THE REST THE SAME WAY YOU WOULD FOR THE ORIGINAL BONELESS TANDOORI ROLL.

TANDOORI CHICKEN ROLLS

 SHAUN & SAMANTHA

YOU'LL NEED:

1 free-range chicken, deboned

250 ml Bulgarian yogurt

juice of 2 lemons

a big handful of fresh coriander

about 3 garlic cloves, crushed and chopped

1 tablespoon of ground cumin seeds

about 1 teaspoon of ground coriander

½ teaspoon of cayenne pepper or hot chilli powder

¼ teaspoon of ground cardamom

¼ teaspoon of freshly grated nutmeg

¼ teaspoon of ground cloves

a splash of olive oil – if the mixture is too thick, add an extra couple of splashes

¼ teaspoon of red dye (optional)

a good pinch of cracked black pepper

a couple of pinches of coarse sea salt

butcher's string

Once you've deboned the chicken like a pro, cut it into halves (each half should have a breast, thigh and drumstick). Trim off any excess fat, but make sure that the skin covering the chicken is still intact – it will help to keep the chicken moist when you braai it. Also skewer some holes into the chicken before you pop it into the marinade so that it will better absorb the flavour.

To prepare the marinade, combine the remainder of the ingredients in a large mixing bowl except for the fresh coriander. The marinade is spot on if it has a similar consistency to hummus, so if it's a little bit too thick, add a splash of olive oil. Put the deboned chicken halves on their backs, then spread a thick layer of marinade onto them and break a small handful of coriander onto both halves. Roll the drumstick and thigh into the breast, and tie the roll up tightly using string. Make sure you use a bit of muscle to really secure the roll. Do the same with the other half of the chicken then pop both rolls into the marinade, massaging the meat and making sure it's completely covered with the sauce. Cover the bowl with cling wrap and pop it in the fridge to marinate overnight.

BRAAI TIME

Braai the rolls over moderate coals, turning them every five minutes – think of a rotisserie being turned slowly. If the coals run out of oomph (like a certain rugby team, who I'd rather not mention – Pretoria okes are big!) then rather take the rolls off the heat, add a couple more logs and wait for the fire to be the right temperature again. Once the chicken is done to perfection, cut the rolls into 2 cm-thick slices and you're ready to eat. Serve and enjoy with the compliments that will be thrown your way. And maybe some rice and salad.

THERE IS SOMETHING VERY SOUTH AFRICAN ABOUT MAKING A MIELIE ON THE BRAAI. THE SMOKY FLAVOUR THE BRAAI IMPARTS, COMBINED WITH LASHINGS OF CREAMY SALTED BUTTER MELTED ALL OVER THE MIELIE (AND YOUR CHIN), IS JUST ABSOLUTE UMAMI MAGIC.

ROLLED BUTTERED MIELIES

 JUSTIN BONELLO

Not THAT 'buttered mielie', you dodgy Durbanites! (Thanks, John Bennett.)

Not sure how many of you guys have tried this, but this is my new version of the perfect buttered mielie. All you need is a wooden board, some braaied mielies and a selection of flavoured butters your friends can roll their mielies in. Play around with this and see what flavour combinations you like. Or just copy me:

Mix soft butter with:

★ Chopped spring onion, fresh coriander, chilli and grated Parmesan.

★ Paprika, chopped parsley, ground cumin, chilli powder and cracked black pepper.

★ Lemon zest, lemon juice, cream cheese, basil pesto and cracked black pepper.

★ Chopped mint, crushed garlic and crumbled feta.

Once you've got your butter ready and the mielies have been braaied to perfection, put the butter on a wooden chopping board and roll the mielie over it until covered. Then tuck in! Or just go traditional and drop dollops of butter on top of the mielies and let it melt. How you manage to remove the kernels that get stuck in your teeth is your problem ...

IF YOU DON'T KNOW HOW TO CUT CHICKEN INTO BRAAI PIECES, GO TO PAGE 22, BUT IF YOU DO, GO AHEAD AND DO THAT FIRST. IF YOU CAN'T BE BOTHERED, BUY SOME READY-CUT PIECES … BUT JUST KNOW THAT IF YOU DO, YOU'LL LOSE SOME SERIOUS BRAAI KUDOS.

ORIENTAL-STYLE CHICKEN

 MARTHINUS FERREIRA

Mix all the ingredients together (except the chicken and lemon grass) and blitz them in a blender. If you don't have one, crush the fennel seeds, finely chop up everything else and mix it all together, before adding the lemon grass. Pour this marinade over the chicken pieces in a big bowl, cover with cling wrap and let it rest in the fridge for anything from 24 to 48 hours.

Braai on medium coals, starting with the breasts and thighs first and adding the drumsticks and the chicken wings later – they cook faster. All in all, the chicken shouldn't take longer than 45 minutes to cook through.

YOU'LL NEED:

1 free-range chicken, cut into braai pieces

1 lemon grass stalk, bruised and chopped up

3 garlic cloves, crushed and chopped

2 chillies, chopped

a large chunk of ginger, grated

a handful of fresh coriander

a small handful of sweet basil, chopped

50 ml fish sauce

about 1 tablespoon of fennel seeds

a splash of canola oil

5 ml sesame seed oil

juice of 2 lemons and 3 limes

a couple of pinches of salt and cracked black pepper

 A DIPPING SAUCE (page 110), COCONUT FRIED RICE (page 177) and FRIED BREAD (page 33). Dunk your chicken into the dipping sauce and chow down.

YOU KNOW THAT SCENE IN A MOVIE WHEN THE TYPICAL AFRICAN AMERICAN FAMILY GOES HOME AFTER CHURCH TO LIGHT UP THE 'BARBECUE' AND MAKE PLATES AND PLATES OF OH-SO-GOOD SOUL FOOD FOR ABOUT A THOUSAND OF THEIR CLOSEST FRIENDS? IT'S MOVIE SCENES LIKE THIS THAT MAKE ME CRAVE REAL SOUL FOOD.

THIS IS MARTHINUS'S VERSION OF FRIED BREAD, AND IT'S GREAT WITH ANY TYPE OF CHICKEN (PAGES 26, 28 AND 30) OR SHORT AND STICKY RIBS (PAGE 166). IN MY OPINION, FRIED BREAD DESERVES A SPOT ON A TABLE IN THE MIDDLE OF YOUR GARDEN, WITH CONVERSATIONS (AND WINE) FLOWING AND GOOD MUSIC PLAYING IN THE BACKGROUND, DURING A SUNDAY LUNCH ON A SUMMER'S AFTERNOON.

F R I E D   B R E A D

 MARTHINUS FERREIRA

In a large bowl, mix the cake flour, yeast and sugar together by hand – you're spot on if the dough is still very sticky. Cover with a damp tea towel and leave to double in size for about 45 minutes to an hour. (I'll leave it up to you to figure out how to get the sticky dough off your hands.) Once the dough has doubled, knock it down, pour about 100 ml of olive oil into the bottom of a round baking tin and swirl it around to make sure you grease the entire tin. Put the dough into the baking tin, and with greased hands, push the dough so it reaches all the edges of the tin. Leave the dough to rise again while you get your fire ready.

After the dough has proofed (fancy word for risen), you can virtually top it with anything you like. Marthinus chose olives, a selection of fresh herbs, onions and tomatoes, seasoned with coarse salt and cracked black pepper. I'm thinking rosemary, garlic and coarse sea salt, but it's totally up to you.

Next, grab some foil, shape it into three balls (about the size of golf balls) and place them inside the bottom of the potjie. Rest the baking tin on top of the foil. This will help to prevent the bottom of the bread from burning. Place the potjie pot straight onto moderate coals, pop the lid on and scatter a couple of coals over the top to create the ultimate potjie oven. Bake on top of moderate coals for about 30 to 45 minutes, or until the bread is cooked through and beautifully golden on top. Take it off the fire and slice the bread in the same way you would cut a pie.

Brothers and sisters ... you don't have to go to church. You've just arrived in heaven!

YOU'LL NEED:

500 g cake flour

20 g instant yeast, mixed with 280 ml lukewarm water and left until frothy – about ten minutes

5 g sugar

100 ml olive oil

a round baking tin or deep enamel plate that will fit into a flat-bottomed potjie

a roll of foil

THERE ARE SOME THINGS IN LIFE THAT JUST WORK. A HOT COFFEE AND HOME-MADE RUSK AT SUNRISE. A COLD BEER AT SUNSET. AND IN-BETWEEN? A DECENT, CRUNCHY COLESLAW AND BRAAIED CHICKEN LUNCH ON A LAZY DAY. IN FACT, IF YOU CAN HAVE ALL OF THIS IN ONE DAY, I'D SAY YOU'RE HAVING A PRETTY GOOD TIME. AND IF YOU MANAGE TO DO ALL OF THIS SOMEWHERE IN THE GREAT OUTDOORS WHERE THE ONLY NOISES YOU HEAR ARE YOUR OWN THOUGHTS AND A FRIEND PLAYING GUITAR IN THE BACKGROUND, YOU ARE DEFINITELY ON TOP OF THE WORLD.

SOUTHERN-STYLE SLAW

 JUSTIN BONELLO

YOU'LL NEED:

about half a head of a big cabbage, finely shredded

a couple of carrots, finely chopped or grated

about half an onion, finely chopped

a handful of fresh fennel, finely chopped

2 big dollops of crème fraîche

a good squeeze of lemon juice

a splash of white vinegar

salt and cracked black pepper, to taste

If you know how to make mayonnaise, do that. If you don't, then I urge you to buy good quality mayo, otherwise you might as well just go buy some ready-made coleslaw that's been sitting in the same container for weeks. You guys know how I feel about junk food!

Okay, speech done, this is what you do:

Mix together the shredded cabbage, chopped carrots, onion, fennel, mayonnaise, crème fraîche, a proper squeeze of lemon juice, a splash of white vinegar, salt and cracked black pepper. Pop it into the fridge and let it sit for an hour to allow all those lekker flavours to develop.

 PERI-PERI SPATCHCOCK (page 26) and FRIED BREAD (page 33). Finger-licking good ... **for real.**

LESOTHO

MOUNTAIN KINGDOM

If you're South African and you've never been to the mountain kingdom of Lesotho, you've never truly lived. Beyond the fact that it is one of the friendliest countries in the world, with cries of 'Lumela!' echoing through the valleys and vales, it's a country that looks like a giant's vast playground and is one of the most beautiful rural parts of Africa. Once you've been there, it will get under your skin ... forever.

There are loads of border crossings into the mountain kingdom. We went in (and out) at Maseru Bridge. My advice? Get out of the chaos of the capital city Maseru as soon as possible, and be warned: like many of our neighbouring countries, there are no real road rules yet there are roadblocks everywhere.

We spent our week in Lesotho at the Malealea Lodge (roughly 90 km from Maseru), and driving there is an adventure in itself – you can't go faster than about 10 km per hour in 4x4 mode for the last stretch, especially if it's raining. Chances are, if you do, that you'll go off a cliff. Life in Lesotho is all about taking it slow so that you can experience a real taste of Basotho life.

The moment you escape the hustle and bustle, it will feel like you can touch the sky, so roll down the car windows (maybe not in the middle of winter though) and breathe it all in as you snake your way through the mountains, past the villages and the kaleidoscope of yellow, red and orange sandstone cliffs. Visiting this humble land – a place without fences – will be the experience of a lifetime and because there are less than 2 million people in Lesotho, there's a lot of space to explore.

PONY TREKKING

Horses aren't indigenous to southern Africa, yet in the mountain kingdom of Lesotho, a virtual paradise with remote villages that are barely accessible by car, horses have ruled for almost 200 years, and when you go to Lesotho, you'll understand why. A horse (or in our case, a Basotho pony) can go where no car could ever dream of going.

It's one of the most mountainous regions in Africa and if you want to meet the warm-hearted rural people of Lesotho, there are only two ways to do it. One is by foot and the other is by horse. I suggest horse.

My only advice? When you go uphill, lean forward and when you're going down, lean back. And my last bit of advice? Just remember to pray (to whoever is out there) because there'll be some moments when you'll feel like you're defying death.

It will be one of the best experiences of your life.

S E S O T H O

I FOUND SOME BASIC SESOTHO PHRASES IN ONE OF
THE BOOKS LYING AROUND AT THE LODGE. IT'S PRETTY
HANDY – ESPECIALLY WHEN YOU WANT TO VISIT THE
LOCAL VILLAGES … AND YOU REALLY SHOULD.

HELENA (MY WRITER) AND I ARE AT A BIT OF A WAR
WITH THE FIRST WORD 'HELLO'. SHE SAYS IT'S 'LUMELA'
WHEN YOU'RE IN LESOTHO, AND 'DUMELA' IN SOUTH
AFRICA. I SAY IT'S 'DUMELA' EVERYWHERE. YOU CAN
DECIDE WHO TO BELIEVE.

Hello! *LUMELA! / DUMELA!*
Yes. *E-EA.*
No. *CHE.*
How are you? *LE KAE?*
I am well, thank you. *KE PHELA HANGLE, KEA LEBOHA.*
What is your name? *LEBITSO LA HAU U MANG?*
Where are you going? *U EAKAE?*
I am sore. *KE BOHLOKO.*
I am tired. *KE KHATETSE.*
Let's go. *A RE'ENG.*
Hurry up! *POTLAKA!*
It's beautiful. *E NTLE.*
Horse. *PERE.*
Dog. *NTJA.*
Cat. *KATSE.*
Pig. *FARIKE.*

DURING THE AUDITION ROUNDS FOR SEASON 2 OF *ULTIMATE BRAAI MASTER* I MET THE BERRY BRIGHT FOOD FANATICS, WHO HAD TRAVELLED ALL THE WAY FROM THE KAROO TO COMPETE IN CAPE TOWN. THEY MADE THIS TONGUE AND TAIL POTJIE AND IT SECURED A SPOT IN MY MEMORY (FOREVER) AND A SPOT ON THE ROAD TRIP OF A LIFETIME. MY POINT? *THAT'S* HOW GOOD IT IS! THIS POTJIE SHOULD DEFINITELY GO ONTO YOUR DINNER TABLE FOR A SPECIAL OCCASION!

TONGUE AND TAIL POTJIE

 NICOLE & SUZANNE

★ THE POTJIE

YOU'LL NEED:

6–8 sheep tongues, cleaned and left in salted water overnight – do this the same day you make the curry paste

a glug of olive oil

500 g lamb knuckles

2 kg sheep tails – you can try and get these at your local butcher, but chances are you need to know a Karoo farmer

about 5 garlic cloves, crushed and chopped

2 chunks of ginger, bruised

Worcester sauce

garlic-, ginger- and sesame-flavoured soy sauce

Maldon salt and cracked black pepper

half a bottle of good quality port or red wine

a small packet of baby potatoes, unpeeled

about 2 handfuls of pickling onions, peeled

a packet of baby carrots

a small handful of fresh rosemary

★ CURRY PASTE

Make this the night before the big event and store in an airtight container.

YOU'LL NEED:

2 heaped tablespoons of medium to hot curry powder

2 teaspoons of turmeric

2 teaspoons of ground coriander

3 teaspoons of ground cumin

4 whole star anise

1 tablespoon of whole mustard seeds, ground

1 tablespoon of garam masala

6–8 curry leaves

4–6 cinnamon sticks

1 stalk of dried lemon grass, bruised and chopped

1 dried chilli, chopped

a splash of red wine vinegar

about ¾ cup of apricot jam

2 teaspoons of sugar

Mix everything together to form a paste. Dip your finger in and if it tastes too sweet, add more vinegar. Too sour? Add more sugar.

Once you've successfully browned the meat like a pro (I hope), the Berry Bright ladies advise layering the vegetables on top then pouring over the curry paste. They say that you have to press down on the vegetables with the back of a wooden spoon to ensure that the curry paste mixes with the rest of the pot. I say stir the curry paste into the potjie first, and then start layering vegetables on top. Put a couple of sprigs of fresh rosemary on top of the vegetables, then pop the lid back on. Simmer gently on a low heat for another hour and a half until the potatoes are cooked. NEVER ever stir the pot. If you notice that there's not enough liquid while it's cooking, add a splash of water every now and then, but be very careful not to drown the vegetables! It's potjiekos ... not soup!

★ THE BERRIES' CHERRY TWIST

About 40 minutes before you're going to start dishing up the potjie, wrap maraschino cherries in bacon and let them lie in brandy for about half an hour. Then braai them over moderate coals until crispy.

Serve the potjie on top of rice, garnished with fresh parsley and cherries. Eat until you fall over!

Bring a pot of salted water to the boil, add the sheep tongues and simmer for about an hour. Take them out and keep to the side. Pour the water out of the potjie. Put the potjie back over the fire, pour in a decent glug of olive oil and pop in the knuckles, tails, garlic, ginger, a couple of splashes of Worcester sauce and loads of soy sauce. Stir every now and then, frying the meat until it's brown. Once this is done, put the sheep tongues back into the pot and fry for another 15 minutes, stirring often. Season with salt and pepper, then add about half a bottle of port or red wine. Reduce the heat, put the lid on and simmer very gently for about an hour and a half, or until the meat starts to soften. There has to be enough liquid in the pot during this cooking time otherwise the meat will burn ... and I promise you, once that happens, the whole potjie will taste of burnt meat and it'll be ruined. You won't be very popular, so keep an eye on it.

PAP IS A FAVOURITE STAPLE FOOD FOR MANY SOUTH AFRICANS, AND WHEN YOU SERVE IT WITH GOOD OLD BRAAIVLEIS, AND A NICE SPICY CHAKALAKA, SOMETHING HAPPENS WHERE YOU CAN'T HELP BUT EAT WITH YOUR HANDS ... WELL AT LEAST THAT'S WHAT HAPPENS TO ME! BUT AS POPULAR AS PAP IS, SO MANY PEOPLE JUST DON'T GET IT RIGHT. HERE'S A RECIPE FOR FAIL-PROOF PAP AND SOME OF THE BEST CHAKALAKA I'VE HAD THE PLEASURE OF DUNKING MY PAP INTO. PLEASE DON'T BE CHEAP AND BUY IT IN A CAN! IT'S EASY TO MAKE AND THE DIFFERENCE BETWEEN HOME-MADE CHAKALAKA AND THE TINNED VERSION SIMPLY PLONKED NEXT TO YOUR PAP IS HUGE.

PAP AND CHAKALAKA

 JUSTIN BONELLO

★ THE CHAKALAKA

YOU'LL NEED:

about ¾ cup of canola oil (really!)

a big chunk of ginger, finely chopped

3 garlic cloves, crushed and chopped

3 or 4 green chillies, chopped

1 onion, finely chopped

1 heaped tablespoon of red curry paste – if you like it seriously hot, add more

5–6 big beefy tomatoes, chopped

a couple of carrots, peeled and grated

1 green pepper, coarsely chopped

about half a cabbage, shredded

salt and cracked black pepper, to taste

Put a fireproof saucepan or potjie over moderate coals. Heat up the oil then add the ginger, garlic, chilli and onion, and fry until the onion is soft. Stir in the curry paste and fry for another couple of minutes. Next, add the chopped tomatoes and let the mixture cook for a couple more minutes. Stir in the grated carrots, chopped green pepper, shredded cabbage and salt and pepper. Take the saucepan (or potjie) off the heat and let it cool down completely – the idea is that the veggies will still be nice and crunchy. If you leave the chakalaka to develop overnight it will taste even better the next day.

★ KRUMMELPAP (CRUMBLY PORRIDGE)

YOU'LL NEED:
salt
1 litre of boiling water
4 cups of maize meal
a knob of butter, to serve
cracked black pepper, to taste

Add salt to the boiling water then pour the maize meal into the middle of the pot (roughly in the shape of a pyramid). Put the lid on and simmer gently for about ten to 20 minutes to let the grains swell. Take a big two-pronged fork (the kind you stick into a big roast beef when you're about to carve it) and stir the dry maize meal from the middle to the sides. The idea is to keep the pap as crumbly as possible, so when you do this, there shouldn't be a lot of water left in the pot, otherwise you'll end up with big lumps instead of crumbs. Pop the lid back on and let it cook slowly for another 20 minutes, then take that same fork and stir it again. Put the lid on once more and leave the pap to steam for another 20 minutes on low heat. Stir in a knob of butter and some cracked black pepper just before serving. This is also great as a breakfast, served with butter, milk and sugar.

★ STYWE PAP (STIFF PORRIDGE)

This is the best type of pap to serve with chakalaka and meat – scoop it up with your fingertips and dunk it into the chakalaka. Yum.

YOU'LL NEED:
4 cups of water
a couple of pinches of salt
2½ cups of maize meal

Pour the water into a potjie pot and bring to the boil. Add a couple of pinches of salt and vigorously stir in the maize meal. Cover with the lid, reduce the heat of the coals by scraping some to the side and simmer over low coals for about 30 to 40 minutes.

I LOVE A GOOD LAMB CHOP, BRAAIED TO CRISPY PERFECTION, WHERE YOU START BY BITING INTO THE FATTY SIDE OF THE CHOP AND END UP ALMOST GNAWING ON THE BONE (HAMSTER STYLE), SCRAPING OFF EVERY LAST BIT OF MEAT YOU MANAGE TO GET YOUR TEETH ON. NOT A PRETTY PICTURE, I ADMIT, BUT WHO HASN'T DONE THIS BEFORE? IT'S DELICIOUS. PROBLEM IS, A LOT OF PEOPLE GET THE LAMB CHOP WRONG – AND I DON'T BLAME YOU, BECAUSE WHAT YOU'RE TRYING TO DO IS GET THE FAT CRISPY, BUT WHILE ATTEMPTING TO DO THAT, YOU COMPLETELY OVERCOOK THE MEAT. CRISPY FAT AND DRY MEAT IS NOT THE BEST COMBINATION. LUCKY FOR YOU, I HAVE THE SOLUTION, AND IN TURN, I URGE YOU TO HELP ONE LAMB-CHOP-LOVING FRIEND AT A TIME.

THE PERFECT LAMB CHOP

 JUSTIN BONELLO

FOR SIX PEOPLE, YOU'LL NEED:
12 Karoo lamb loin chops
4 sprigs of rosemary – at least 10 cm in length
coarse sea salt
cracked black pepper

I don't believe in marinating lamb chops ... if you get proper Karoo lamb chops, the lambs already marinated themselves when they ate all those fragrant Karoo bossies. The meat should speak for itself. So the first thing you do is make a fire and wait for the coals to be at a moderate to low heat.

To complete the perfect lamb chop experience (and to save on having to wash any cutlery later) serve these beauties with pap and spicy chakalaka (page 42) and braai broodjies (page 80). When you bite into that lamb chop, you'll get it. Crispy fat, and tender, delicious and juicy meat that isn't burnt.

Good old braaivleis at its best ...

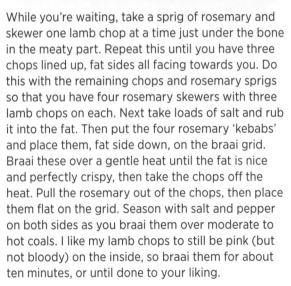

While you're waiting, take a sprig of rosemary and skewer one lamb chop at a time just under the bone in the meaty part. Repeat this until you have three chops lined up, fat sides all facing towards you. Do this with the remaining chops and rosemary sprigs so that you have four rosemary skewers with three lamb chops on each. Next take loads of salt and rub it into the fat. Then put the four rosemary 'kebabs' and place them, fat side down, on the braai grid. Braai these over a gentle heat until the fat is nice and perfectly crispy, then take the chops off the heat. Pull the rosemary out of the chops, then place them flat on the grid. Season with salt and pepper on both sides as you braai them over moderate to hot coals. I like my lamb chops to still be pink (but not bloody) on the inside, so braai them for about ten minutes, or until done to your liking.

MANY OF YOU MIGHT NOT BE AWARE OF THIS, BUT AFTER SOUTH AFRICANS, ARGENTINIANS HAVE BRAAIS (BUT NOT RUGBY) DOWN TO A FINE ART AND HAVE BEEN SPIT-BRAAIING OVER OPEN FIRES FOR CENTURIES. WE HAD TWO DAYS TO LET OUR HAIR DOWN WHILE WE WERE IN LESOTHO, SO WE DEVELOPED THE IDEA FOR AN ASADO SPIT BRAAI (AND AN EXCUSE FOR A PARTY THAT LASTED UNTIL FIVE THE NEXT MORNING). IF YOU WANT AN EXCUSE TO HAVE A PARTY FOR LOADS OF HUNGRY PEOPLE, BUT YOU'RE TIRED OF THE TYPICAL CHOP-EN-DOP SCENARIO, THEN I SUGGEST YOU DO THIS.

ASADO AL PALO!

THE BASIC IDEA OF THIS SPIT

I'm not going to give a step-by-step on how to put this together. Have a look at the photos and figure it out. It's actually quite simple, so call on your inner MacGyver. If you make a decent one, it will last you the rest of your life.

★ Three pieces of flat iron, about 2 cm wide and just under 1 cm thick.

★ For the long bar, this flat iron should be between 1.5–1.8 m long.

★ The two crossbars should both be just under 1 m long.

After you've built your spit like an expert, and once you've decided which type of meat to use (we did goat, lamb and piggy … it was a big crowd), open the carcass, wash the meat thoroughly with water and wipe it dry with a paper towel. Put the spit on a clean flat surface, and attach the legs to the top and bottom crossbars with wire. Do the same to the centre of the carcass, then carry it to the fire (you'll definitely need some help with this!). Balance the spit at a 45-degree angle over moderate coals, with the inside of the carcass towards the heat first. If any part of the carcass starts to burn during the cooking time, it's a good idea to cover it with foil.

How long you braai the meat for depends on how hot your coals are, the consistency of the heat and, of course, the size of the carcass. A lamb of 10 kg takes about three to four hours to cook through and a 'big fatso' weighing in at 20 kg takes about five to six hours. Another easy way to test if it's ready is to use a meat thermometer: stick it into the thickest part of the meat; if the temperature reaches 65 °C, it means your meat is medium and if it reads 70 °C it's well done. Once the meat is cooked to your liking, carve it straight off the spit. If you start carving the meat and notice it's still rare to the bone, braai it some more.

 SERVE WITH A selection of salads, TORTILLAS (page 87) and fillings – think tzatziki, relish, guacamole and so on.

So before you start, attach the lamb (±18kg) to the spit, then, hose down thoroughly to make sure it's clean. While it's still moist, give it a good rub with the following mix:
Handful (big) of dried oregano; handful (big) of rock salt, handful (big) of crushed garlic & finally, the juice of five lemons. If this isn't enough to coat the whole lamb, make more. You can use the leftovers for the basting sauce. Cook for 5-8 hours until the shoulder blades start pulling out, making sure to move MORE coals around the thicker parts of the lamb, otherwise the lamb will be raw on the bone. 30 minutes before you want to carve and serve, baste the lamb every 5 minutes with a sauce made by combining the following: 1 litre of lemon juice, big handful of oregano, big handful of rock salt and a couple of heads of crushed garlic.

The recipe was given 2 me by my wife's godfather Panno, and it's now virtually the only way i'll cook a whole lamb, tried, tested and bloody delicious.....

HEIDI'S GOAT (MARTHINUS)

BASTING SAUCE:

5 Blocks of Butter
└ Melt & Mix with:

2 × 1.5l Olive Oil
— Not Virgin!!

1 Bulb of Garlic
— Peeled + Crushed

150g Coarse Sea Salt
The juice of 8 Big Lemons
A handful of Fresh Rosemary - chopped
A handful of Fresh Thyme - chopped
A caple of Bay Leaves
4 TBS Paprika
4 TBS (Ground) Coriander
4 whole dried Chillies — chopped

** SALT THE GOAT BEFORE
PUTTING IT ON THE SPIT **

Once the Goat has been rubbed
with Salt & is on Spit, Braai
& Baste for about 8
hours.
BOOM!

for A 20kg Pig

4 L Water
2 kg Salt.
700g Sugar
fist full of fresh Thyme.
6 Bay leaves
5 Crushed Chilies
Stem Ginger
2 Garlic Bulbs

Bring all the ingredients
To the boil together &
Cool.

flatten & Strap your Pig to the Spit for the Ride of
his life.

lay the Pig over hot Coals for Approximately 8
hours, Continuously turning & Injecting with the Brine

for the final few Minutes of Cooking, Baste the
Swine with the following Mixture.

2 tins Colemans Mustard Powder
3 jars Dijon Mustard 1
1 jar Whole grain Mustard
500g Sugar
500 ml vinager
Chopped Corriander
Chopped Chili
Dash of Smoked paprika

Mix together &
Baste on the
inside of the
Carcass

Ahh Done? Now feast.

LESOTHO
MOUNTAIN KINGDOM

DOUBLE CHOCOLATE CHELSEA BUNS

 CARO

FOR 12 FRIENDS AND A SUGAR-CRAVING DONKEY...

FOR THE DOUGH, YOU'LL NEED:

1 cup of milk, warmed

2 teaspoons of dried yeast

60 ml castor sugar

500 g white bread flour

10 ml salt

100 ml butter, melted

5 ml vanilla essence

1 egg, lightly beaten

sunflower oil

FOR THE FILLING, YOU'LL NEED:

60 ml butter, melted

1 slab of white chocolate, chopped

1 slab of milk chocolate, chopped

150 g almonds, bashed

FOR THE GLAZE, YOU'LL NEED:

45 ml honey, mixed with a drop of hot water

juice of about 2 lemons

375 ml icing sugar, sifted

Warm the milk slightly and gently whisk in the yeast and sugar. Set aside for about ten to 15 minutes or until frothy. Next, sift the flour into a large bowl, add salt and stir through the yeast mixture, melted butter, vanilla essence and whisked egg. Mix until you have a rough dough, then turn the dough onto a lightly floured surface and knead it for about 15 minutes or until smooth and elastic. Lightly grease the ball of dough with sunflower oil, put it in a large bowl, cover it, put it in a warm spot and leave it to double in size – for about an hour.

Roll the dough out on a floured surface into a large rectangular shape, about 2 cm thick. Brush with half the melted butter and scatter all the chocolate and half the nuts.

Now roll the longer side of the rectangular dough into a cigar / sausage shape. Cut into 12 equal pieces. Turn each piece on its side and arrange in a butter-greased, flat-bottomed potjie, leaving a little space between each spiral roll. Cover and leave to rise for another hour (Caro's code for: go sit under a tree and have a drink). After about an hour (or two tall drinks) the rolls should be puffy and have squeezed together.

Brush with the remaining melted butter and honey (loosened with a little hot water) and scatter the leftover nuts on top. Cover with the potjie lid, top with a few coals and bake for about 25 to 30 minutes over medium to cool coals (think 180 °C) until golden and cooked through. Take it off the heat, let the buns cool slightly then mix lemon juice and sifted icing sugar together. Drizzle over the buns before serving. Go get a picnic blanket, find a spot in the sun, make some good coffee and grab your friends. This is the perfect way to end a lazy winter's afternoon. If you're at Malealea Lodge, watch out for the donkey! His name is Chester and he's got a serious sweet tooth!

THE EVENTS BY 707 ENTERTAINMENT

• MISS AFRICA BEAUTY PAGEANT
• MISS LOVELY LEGS PAGEANT
• MISS SOWETO PAGEANT
• MR SOWETO PAGEANT......

SOWETO

PANYAZA 707 CLUB: HEITA! HOLA!

Johannesburg is the biggest man-made forest in Africa, is home to millions of South Africans and is the economic powerhouse known to most as the City of Gold. This mainstream destination is definitely a far cry from all the naturally breathtaking rural environments we had travelled to so far. But keep in mind that this was not only a road trip. It was also a braai adventure, and one of the best adventures you can have with braaivleis is going to one of the many incredible shisa nyama joints scattered in and around South Africa's townships. After Mzoli's in Gugulethu on the outskirts of Cape Town, the next best thing is Panyaza, situated in the hustle and bustle of Soweto. I promise you, if you've never been to one of these joints, you've never experienced the street culture of South Africa's favourite pastime.

When we arrived we were greeted by a local doing doughnuts with his souped-up BMW in the middle of the street – his screeching tyres giving off smoke of a less pleasant kind. At the door there was a sign that warned us not to enter with our cars (seemed logical, but maybe a warning the BMW guy had a problem with). Once inside, our senses had to adjust to thick dark braai smoke hanging heavily under the roof of the lapa and, in complete contrast, a scattering of flamingo-pink chairs and tables – a strange choice in décor that would be out of place in any restaurant ... but not Panyaza.

This is definitely Jozi's best braai restaurant – a place where you order big drinks, eat big food and shake it up to deep house beats all day long. And don't ask for cutlery – here you eat with your hands, sauce dripping down your elbows and chin. This will happen, and when it does, wipe your hands on your jeans, order another drink and get dirty. Speaking of ... if you find yourself legless after a day of partying, you can rent a room for the night ... or even for just an hour (but common sense tells me that these rooms aren't used for sleeping, so maybe take a taxi home instead). Oh, and before you leave, buy a 'Panyaza Addict' T-shirt to show your friends that, for one day, you had a taste of real kasi life!

PARMESAN BISCUITS
WITH CREAM CHEESE,
BILTONG AND SWEET
CHILLI SAUCE

ZESTY SPICY
ROASTED NUTS

IN THE SPIRIT OF A GOOD PARTY, THE FOLLOWING
RECIPES ARE ALL EASY PARTY FOOD. ENJOY!

BRAAI SNACKS

BY JANET

POTATO
SKINS WITH
HORSERADISH
AND BACON
DIP

BRAAI SNACKS

YOU KNOW HOW I ALWAYS SAY THAT BRAAI CULTURE IN SOUTH AFRICA TRANSLATES INTO A BIG KUIER? AND THAT SOMETIMES THAT BIG KUIER TURNS A LITTLE MESSY? IF YOU'RE SOUTH AFRICAN, YOU DEFINITELY KNOW HOW IT GOES SOMETIMES: THE FIRE GETS STARTED A LITTLE TOO LATE (TRADITION), FRIENDS SNACK ON MSG-FILLED CRISPS TO KEEP THEM GOING (BAD HABIT), AND BY THE TIME THE BRAAI IS READY, SOME OF YOUR FRIENDS (YOU KNOW THE ONES) ARE SLIGHTLY TIPSY AND DEBATING RUGBY, RELIGION AND POLITICS (THREE BIG CONVERSATIONAL NO-NOS AROUND THE FIRE). THIS TYPICAL BRAAI SCENARIO CAN BE AVOIDED WITH A WELL-THOUGHT-OUT (AND MADE-IN-ADVANCE) BRAAI SNACK MENU FOR YOU AND YOUR FRIENDS TO MUNCH ON. IT'S MORE SUBSTANTIAL THAN OILY CRISPS AND SHOULD KEEP THEIR BEHAVIOUR (AND CHOLESTEROL LEVELS) IN CHECK WHILE THEY (PATIENTLY) WAIT FOR THE LAST LAMB CHOP TO BE BRAAIED AND THAT DAMN POTATO BAKE TO BE READY ALREADY! BECAUSE THESE ARE BEFORE-THE-BRAAI SNACKS, YOU CAN MAKE THEM IN THE COMFORT OF YOUR KITCHEN (SCORE!).

★ POTATO SKINS WITH HORSERADISH AND BACON DIP ★

This is a great snack to make if you happen to have peeled potatoes for something you're making for dinner (mash, gnocchi – you get the idea) and you don't know what to do with the leftover skins. Make sure the skin still has some flesh on it.

Using a paring knife, carefully peel the potato skins into thick strips, about ½–1 cm thick. Bring some water to the boil, pop the peels into the water and cook for a couple of minutes. This helps to reduce the amount of starch in the skins.

Take them off the heat and then drain the skins on a kitchen towel to soak up the excess moisture. Once cooled and relatively dry, toss them in the seasoned cornflour and set aside. Heat up a pot of oil, carefully put the skins into the hot oil (don't burn yourself!) and deep-fry until cooked through and golden. Drain on more kitchen towels and serve hot with the dip.

While the potato skins are deep-frying, grab a non-stick pan and fry the chopped bacon and rosemary until crisp. Stir through the garlic and chilli flakes, fry for a couple of extra seconds, remove from the heat and drain on a kitchen towel.

Mix the cream cheese with a squeeze of lemon juice and enough sour cream to form a thick, easy-to-scoop dip. Mix in half the bacon and chives, creamed horseradish and season to taste. Scatter with the remaining bacon and a few extra chopped chives. Dip in with the crispy potato skins.

THE SKINS
YOU'LL NEED:

8–10 large potatoes, scrubbed clean

cornflour, seasoned with salt and pepper

1 bottle of sunflower or canola oil

THE DIP
YOU'LL NEED:

6–8 bacon rashers, chopped

2 teaspoons of rosemary, finely chopped

about ½ tablespoon of dried chilli flakes

2 garlic cloves, crushed

1 tub of cream cheese

¼–⅓ cup of creamed horseradish, depending on your taste

a squeeze of lemon juice

a couple of dollops of sour cream

a big handful of chopped chives

salt and cracked black pepper

PARMESAN BISCUITS
★ WITH CREAM CHEESE, BILTONG ★
AND SWEET CHILLI SAUCE

YOU'LL NEED:

210 g cake flour

½ teaspoon of baking powder

½ teaspoon of paprika

a big pinch of cayenne pepper, ground cumin and ground coriander

a decent pinch of salt

a couple of cracks of black pepper

165 g softened unsalted butter

165 g Parmesan (or any other hard cheese that you like)

1 egg, whisked

really good thick-cut, fatty and moist biltong

a tub of cream cheese

good old sweet chilli sauce

In a large mixing bowl, sift together the flour, baking powder, paprika, cayenne pepper, cumin and coriander, and season with salt and black pepper. Mix the butter with the Parmesan cheese then add it to the dry ingredients. Knead and mix until you've got soft dough, then put it on a clean, floured surface. Roll the dough into a log shape about 5–6 cm in diameter, then cover the log in cling wrap and pop it into the fridge for about 30 minutes to an hour. Preheat the oven to 170 °C and line a baking tray with baking paper. Take the (now firm) dough out the fridge and cut it into thin discs about 1.5 cm thick. Arrange the discs on the baking paper (making sure they don't touch each other) and bake for about 12 minutes or until gold and crispy. Let them cool down then taste a couple of biscuits (cook's advantage) and store them in an airtight container until you're going to use them.

TIP: The beauty of this recipe is that you can freeze the logs and use them whenever the craving hits.

The day your friends and family are coming to the braai, take the biscuits out. Put a generous dollop of cream cheese on each, top with a thick slice of moist and fatty biltong and drizzle with sweet chilli sauce. Make sure you eat a couple of them before you take them out to the braai – these babies disappear in the wink of an eye.

★ ZESTY SPICY ROASTED NUTS ★

THESE ARE SO ADDICTIVE – SO MAKE LOADS OF THEM AND STORE THEM IN YOUR PANTRY OR CUPBOARD FOR WHEN YOU FEEL LIKE A SNACK. ALSO, THIS IS THE EASIEST SNACK IN THE WORLD, SHORT OF BUYING IT AT THE SHOPS – WHICH YOU CAN'T.

Preheat your oven to about 260 °C, toss all the ingredients together in a bowl then spread the mixture out over a baking tin (lined with a baking sheet). Bake the nuts for about eight to ten minutes, toss them around and bake for another eight to ten minutes or until golden. (Warning: watch your nuts! They go from golden brown to black and burnt in a heartbeat.)

Once they're baked to perfection, take them out the oven and try your best not to sneak a couple – you'll burn your lips, fingers and tongue! Let the nuts cool down and store in an airtight container. They should keep for about three months.

YOU'LL NEED:

about 4 cups of raw nuts – whatever tickles your fancy; I used macadamias, pecans, almonds and cashews

juice of 1 lemon

zest of half a lemon

a splash of olive oil

a big pinch of chilli powder

a tablespoon of paprika, smoked or plain

a big pinch of cayenne pepper

a big pinch of ground cumin

a big pinch of ground coriander

½ teaspoon of powdered ginger

a decent pinch of salt

EATING EVERY PART OF THE ANIMAL IS NOTHING NEW (IN SOME CULTURES), AND I'M HAPPY TO SAY THAT IT'S BECOMING MORE AND MORE POPULAR IN MODERN SOCIETY, WITH OFFAL – GIBLETS, KIDNEYS AND INTESTINES – NOW FOUND IN SOME OF SOUTH AFRICA'S BEST RESTAURANTS. WE USED TO EAT ALL OF THIS NOT TOO LONG AGO, BEFORE WE DECIDED IT'S NOT SO LEKKER AS WE THOUGHT IT WAS. BUT NOW OFFAL IS COMING BACK. COOKING THESE DELICACIES IS DEFINITELY NOT FOR THE FAINT OF HEART, BUT I DARE YOU TO TRY. IT MIGHT CHANGE THE WAY YOU LOOK AT MEAT.

WALKIE TALKIE POT

 MARTIN & ZIZA

First up, in a fireproof pan, toast the caraway, coriander and aniseed on moderate coals. Once toasted, let them cool down then grind the seeds in a coffee grinder or bash them as finely as you can with a mortar and pestle. Now, in a large pan, pour in a couple of glugs of sunflower oil and add all the dry ingredients, including the bashed seeds and chopped onions, and fry until all the spices have released their flavours and the onion is cooked.

Bring a separate pot of water to the boil, add the gizzards and simmer until soft. The gizzards should just be covered in water – not completely drowned. Next add the spiced fried onions and the chicken feet, neck and intestines, and simmer until everything is cooked through – about an hour.

In big bowls, garnished with loads of fresh coriander and some fresh bread on the side.

YOU'LL NEED:

6 g caraway seeds

8 g coriander seeds

2 big handfuls of fresh coriander, chopped

3 whole aniseed

a couple of glugs of sunflower oil

2 large onions, chopped

1 tablespoon of chilli flakes

about 1 tablespoon of salt

10 g Rajah medium curry powder

12 g Rajah mild and spicy curry powder

about ½ cup of water

500 g chicken gizzards, seasoned with salt and pepper

500 g chicken feet

500 g chicken neck

200 g chicken intestines – look, I've never come across them, but if you know where to find them, do, and if you don't, leave this out of the recipe

THERE IS SOMETHING BEAUTIFUL ABOUT
A GOOD BURGER. AND ONCE YOU'VE
CONQUERED THAT PERFECT, JUICY
BURGER PATTY, THE SKY'S THE LIMIT.
UNFORTUNATELY, THANKS TO ALL THE FAST
FOOD JOINTS, HAMBURGERS HAVE EARNED
A BAD REPUTATION FOR BEING UNHEALTHY.
IT'S SAD REALLY, BECAUSE WHEN YOU MAKE
YOUR OWN BURGER FROM SCRATCH, YOU ARE
IN CONTROL OF WHAT GOES INTO IT.

CHEESY BACON BURGER

 JUSTIN BONELLO

FOR FIVE BURGERS, YOU'LL NEED:

100 g free-range beef chuck

400 g free-range sirloin

a mincer or food processor

about 1 tablespoon of ground coriander

about 1 tablespoon of ground cumin

about 1 tablespoon of paprika

about 1 tablespoon of dried oregano

1 egg, whisked

a couple of splashes of Worcester sauce

a couple of garlic cloves, crushed and chopped

1 red chilli, seeds removed and finely chopped

Maldon salt and cracked black pepper, to taste

10 rashers of free-range bacon

5 fresh bread rolls

5 slices of cheddar cheese

crispy lettuce, washed and dried

1 red onion, sliced into rings

a couple of ripe tomatoes, sliced

whole-grain mustard

a couple of gherkins, sliced lengthways

Before you start, you should know:

★ The meat is the heart of the burger, so the better quality meat you use, the better the result. The meat-to-fat ratio should ideally be 80% to 20% for the juiciest results. 80% sirloin and 20% beef chuck works well.

★ By grinding your own meat, instead of buying mince at the store, you ensure two things. One, you know exactly what goes into your burger. And two, it'll be a lot more tender than burgers made from store-bought mince. Don't believe me? Test it for yourself!

★ Patties shrink as they cook, so when you shape them, make sure they're slightly bigger in diameter than the bun.

★ Clean the grid properly and brush with oil to help prevent the burgers from sticking while you braai.

★ Don't ever press down on the patties while they're cooking – they'll lose all those lovely juices.

★ About a minute before taking the meat off the grid, cover each with a nice slab of cheddar cheese and let it melt. Once melted, take it off the braai immediately and build the burger – they're best served hot!

⭐ GRIND IT

The first really important thing you need to know is that the meat you use *has* to be cold. The warmer the meat, the softer it becomes, which makes it harder to mince. I've heard that you can even go as far as chilling the grinder in the freezer – but that's completely up to you. Cut the cold beef into cubes about 3 cm x 3 cm. Also make sure that all the connective tissue has been trimmed away. Now mince the beef in batches on a coarse grind. Put it into a bowl, add all the spices, the egg, the Worcester sauce, garlic, chilli, salt and pepper, and mix everything together using your hands. Cover with cling wrap and pop it into the freezer for about 30 to 40 minutes to firm up.

In the meantime, make a sweet barbeque sauce to baste the burger patties with while you're braaiing them. (Recipe is on page 111.)

Next, fry some bacon in a pan over moderate to hot coals. Once the bacon is deliciously crispy, take it off the heat and run back to the kitchen. Now, I have no idea if this actually works, because I never got to taste the burgers I made as my crew devoured them in a matter of minutes, BUT what I did was mix the bacon grease left in the pan with the mince I made earlier. I'm guessing I must have struck gold, because never in my life had I seen burgers being scoffed at such speed. So you can choose to do this or not. Totally up to you. Shape the burgers into five 100 g patties (remember, slightly bigger in diameter than the bun) and you're ready to go.

Get the burger patties on the grid. Moderate to hot coals should do the trick, but if it's too hot, scrape some coals to the side – rather cook your burger for longer than risk burning the one side. About four minutes a side should do the trick – I like my burger medium – but if you prefer it well done, braai it for a couple of minutes longer a side. Keep basting it generously with the barbeque sauce and just before you're about to take it off the heat, top each patty with a slice of cheese and two strips of bacon and let it cook a minute longer.

⭐ BUILD IT

The right balance of crispy lettuce, tangy onions, sweet tomatoes, some whole-grain mustard and gherkin is my idea of the perfect burger, but do whatever you feel like. Just don't ruin it with store-bought tomato sauce or processed cheese.

 Inside paper serviettes and eat outside – a good burger tends to get messy!

WANT SOMETHING FRESH AND FISHY, BUT CAN'T STAND THE THOUGHT OF ANOTHER GREASY PLATEFUL OF FISH AND CHIPS, AND NOT IN THE MOOD FOR SUSHI? JONNO AND KATE'S BURGER IS FRESH, TANGY AND PACKED WITH ALL THE RIGHT FLAVOURS! TRY IT ONCE, YOU'LL LOVE IT FOREVER!

SEARED YELLOWFIN TUNA BURGERS

 KATE & JONNO

> **FOR ONE LUCKY PERSON, YOU'LL NEED:** 1 toasted sesame bun; 1 tuna patty; a good dollop of Asian guacamole; ½ handful of cucumber pickle; about 2 tablespoons of wasabi mayo

★ FOUR 200 G TUNA PATTIES

Cut the tuna loin into chunks and pop them into a large bowl. Mix well with remaining ingredients, except the egg white, then push through a mincer (on the coarsest setting) into a mixing bowl. Knead in the egg white. Mould into about 200 g-sized patties, cover and refrigerate for an hour. Before braaiing, give each patty a brush of soy sauce on either side. Sear on a grid over ridiculously hot coals or in a smoking hot pan for about two minutes a side. Serve rare / blue.

TIP: Do not use a 'sandwich' grid for this. The meat will mush and fall apart. And then so will you.

YOU'LL NEED:

800 g fresh raw yellowfin tuna loin

½ bunch of spring onions, finely chopped

2 big thumbs of ginger, grated finely

3 garlic cloves, finely chopped

zest of 2 limes

50 g coriander, roughly chopped

50 ml Kikkoman soy sauce

4 red chillies, deseeded and finely chopped

1 egg white

a mincer or food processor

★ ASIAN GUACAMOLE

Simply mash the avo with a fork and mix in the remaining ingredients.

1 ripe avocado

a small chunk of ginger, grated

1 garlic clove, crushed and chopped

juice of 1 lime

½ handful of fresh coriander, finely chopped

½ jalapeño, finely chopped

½ red onion, finely diced

salt and cracked black pepper, to taste

★ CUCUMBER PICKLE

Combine all ingredients just before serving for ultimate crunchiness. If you make it too early, the cucumber will go floppy – not so lekker.

½ large cucumber, julienned (fancy word for cutting into thin strips)

2 radishes, julienned

1 celery stick, thinly sliced

1 spring onion, in thin slithers

1 pinch of dry-toasted sesame seeds

a good squeeze of lime juice

2 tablespoons of rice vinegar

a big pinch of sugar

¼ garlic clove, crushed

½ teaspoon of ginger, crushed

a few drops of sesame oil

★ WASABI MAYO

Combine everything and leave for an hour to infuse.

1 cup of good quality mayo – if you know how, make your own

wasabi, to taste

a squeeze of lime

fresh coriander, finely chopped

BUILD THE BURGER, BOB

Bottom roll. Guacamole. Tuna. Cucumber pickle. Wasabi mayo. Top roll. Smash it in your face.

★

THIS IS REALLY EASY PARTY FOOD AND THE BEST PART IS THAT YOUR FRIENDS CAN BUILD THEIR OWN WRAPS. ALL YOU NEED TO DO IS BRAAI THE DUCK AND CUT UP SOME VEGGIES, THEN SIT BACK AND ENJOY THE AFTERNOON.

DUCK WRAPS

 JUSTIN BONELLO

FOR FOUR PEOPLE, YOU'LL NEED:

boiling water

4 duck breasts

Maldon salt

black pepper

about 12 rice-paper wraps

a few bowls of cold water

2 carrots, julienned

½ cucumber, julienned

a couple of spring onions, cut in half and shredded

radishes, finely sliced

chilli, chopped

a couple of chunks of ginger, grated

about 2 handfuls of fresh coriander, torn

toasted sesame seeds (optional)

a bottle of your favourite plum sauce or any sweet sauce you love ... just not chutney

lime wedges, for squeezing

If you've ever attempted to grill duck breasts, you'll know that, because of all the fat and thick skin, the duck tends to be overcooked by the time the fat has been rendered and the skin is nice and crisp. But fear not! There's a simple solution: pour just-boiled water over the skin of the duck breast then score the fat side of the duck with a sharp knife. Now rub Maldon salt and black pepper into the duck breasts. Place the duck, fat side down, straight onto the grid, over moderate coals, and braai for eight to ten minutes. But be careful – if the fire's too hot, the skin will burn. Once the skin is nice and crispy, turn the breasts around and braai the flesh side for another five to eight minutes. Ideally the duck should be medium rare, but once it's done to your liking, take it off the heat and let it rest for a couple of minutes before thinly slicing it up. Put the duck on the table, along with the rice-paper wraps, a couple of bowls of water, some clean tea towels and the assortment of veggies, seeds, lime wedges and plum sauce.

⭐ MAKE YOUR OWN

① Submerge one rice-paper wrap in a bowl of cold water for about a minute or two, until soft.

② Put the rice paper on top of a clean tea towel.

③ Take a little bit of carrot, cucumber, spring onion, radish, chilli and ginger, and arrange them along the centre of the rice-paper round.

④ Top this with some sliced duck, a scattering of fresh coriander and sesame seeds.

⑤ Season with salt and pepper, drizzle with plum sauce and add a squeeze of lime.

⑥ Fold in the one end of the rice paper round, then roll it up firmly and squeeze it closed.

⑦ Enjoy!

BRAAIED PIZZA

 BERTUS BASSON

WAY BACK, WHEN I FIRST STARTED FILMING MY SHOW *COOKED*, I MADE A DUSTBIN PIZZA FOR MY CREW BEFORE WE HIT SPLASHY FEN MUSIC FESTIVAL IN THE SOUTHERN DRAKENSBERG. THAT WAS MY ATTEMPT AT A BRAAIED PIZZA. IN A 45-GALLON METAL DRUM ON TOP OF TWO UNGLAZED TERRACOTTA TILES, I HAD A MAKESHIFT PIZZA OVEN THAT BAKED DELICIOUS PIZZA IN LESS THAN 15 MINUTES. THIS TIME ROUND, BERTUS (A PRO AT SIMPLE AND DELICIOUS FOOD) MADE PIZZA STRAIGHT ON THE BRAAI GRID. I HAD MY DOUBTS, ESPECIALLY AFTER ALL THE EFFORT I WENT TO MAKING A PIZZA OVEN USING A DUSTBIN, BUT ADMITTEDLY HAVE TO SWALLOW MY WORDS. SO TRY THIS IF YOU DON'T HAVE A DUSTBIN LYING AROUND IN YOUR BACKYARD. IT'S WAY SIMPLER. I LOVE LEARNING NEW TRICKS LIKE THIS. BERTUS USES THE SAME BASIC BREAD DOUGH RECIPE THAT I'VE USED FOR YEARS, SO I GUESS IN THE WORLD OF OUTDOOR PIZZA WE'RE EVEN. UNTIL NEXT YEAR ...

FOR THE BEST PIZZA DOUGH, YOU'LL NEED:

500 g white bread flour

a big pinch of salt

10 g yeast

325 ml warm water

Combine the flour and salt in a large mixing bowl. Activate and dissolve the yeast by placing it in another bowl and adding the warm water. Give it a stir, and sprinkle a handful of flour over the mixture to prevent the yeast from forming a crust. Leave the yeast mixture in a warm spot for about ten minutes or until it begins to froth and gradually add it to the flour, mixing it well until it forms a dough. The only way to do this is with your hands. If the dough is too sticky, add a bit more flour; if it's too dry, add a splash more water, and so on. Knead for ten minutes until the dough has a smooth, elastic consistency. Sprinkle some flour onto your work surface, place the dough on the flour and cover with a damp tea towel. Leave the dough to rise for about 30 minutes or until it has doubled in size.

Sprinkle some flour on a clean working surface and tear off a fist-sized piece of dough. Using your fingers or a rolling pin (or a bottle of wine) roll the dough out into your preferred size and shape – keeping in mind it can't be bigger than your braai grid. The border can be slightly thicker if you like a thick crust pizza.

BERTUS DIDN'T DO A TOMATO BASE, BUT USED OLIVE OIL AND SLICED GARLIC INSTEAD.

THIS IS BERTUS'S FAVOURITE TOPPING, BUT THE POSSIBILITIES ARE ENDLESS, SO GO WILD.

YOU'LL NEED:

olive oil, mixed with about 2 garlic cloves, thinly sliced

mozzarella, sliced

red onion, thinly sliced

cherry tomatoes, halved

slices of Parma ham

fresh basil

rocket

Parmesan shavings

salt and cracked black pepper

Take the pizza base and put it on a grid over moderate coals. Braai the base for a couple of minutes, or until the bottom is crispy and golden and the top starts bubbling. Flip the base over and brush the top with the garlicky olive oil. Take out a couple of the garlic slices and arrange them on top of the pizza.

Next, scatter sliced mozzarella on the base – as much as you like. Reduce the heat of your coals slightly by scraping some to the side – the slow heat will give the mozzarella time to melt without burning the bottom of the pizza. Go ahead and drizzle some more garlicky olive oil onto the pizza, then once the cheese has melted, remove the pizza from the heat.

Top with red onion, tomatoes, Parma ham, basil, rocket, Parmesan shavings and season with salt and black pepper.

Cut into odd-sized slices and let your friends dig in (once you've had your slice). Then let them each make their own pizza.

BOOZY FLOATS

 THE CREW

THE TAGLINE OF THIS RECIPE SHOULD BE: 'WHEN YOU WANT ANOTHER DRINK, BUT IT'S TIME FOR DESSERT.' AND WHO DOESN'T LOVE A GOOD OLD ICE CREAM FLOAT? ADD A KICK TO IT AND YOU'VE GOT A WINNER. WHILE SOME OF US WOULD PREFER TO HAVE A MORE DISTINGUISHED DOM PEDRO (PAGE 170) THERE ARE THE HIP (OKAY, OKAY – YOUNGER) ONES WHO GET ABSOLUTELY MESMERISED BY ALL THE DIFFERENT COLOURS OF THE BOOZY FLOATS. PLUS, APPARENTLY IT'S FUN TO TRY AND DRINK IT ALL WITHOUT GETTING BRAIN FREEZE OR MAKING A MESS ON YOUR SHOES. AH, TO BE YOUNG AGAIN! TRY THESE FUN COMBINATIONS OR MAKE UP YOUR OWN.

Coke, brandy and vanilla ice cream.	Cream soda, cane and vanilla ice cream.	Fanta, vodka and vanilla ice cream.

THE RULES

One can of soda, two shots of liquor and two and a half scoops of vanilla ice cream. Serve with a spoon, a straw and a 'jammerlappie' (wet cloth).

⭐

Tsitsikamma is a Khoisan word meaning 'place of much water' and you'll understand why when you're there. It sweeps from the Bloukrans River in the west to Eerste River in the east, has the magnificent Tsitiskamma mountains in the north and is bordered by the Indian Ocean in the south. It's the heart of the Garden Route of the southern Cape and sweeps through 80 km of rugged rocky coastline, evergreen forests and fynbos.

Even though this is the 'adventure capital' of the southern Cape (think zip-lining, bungee jumping, tubing and elephant rides), Tsitsikamma is an area waiting to be explored. Unfortunately it's also the place half of Jo'burg comes to on their December holidays (no offence guys). So my advice? Come in the quieter seasons or, if you live nearby like I do, make a long weekend of it with your family. That way you can explore the area in peace.

EMBRACE THE GREAT OUTDOORS!

If you know even just a little bit about me, you'll probably know that I absolutely live for getting in my car, hitting the open road, rolling down the windows (elbow out, trucker style) and arriving somewhere with a 360-degree view. This is the space where I'm at my happiest. Where I pitch my tent. Where I get to sip whiskey out a bottle around the fire. Where I get to look at the stars. Where I get to breathe. REALLY breathe.

This is how I grew up, and I'm sure this is how many of us remember our holidays as kids. But nowadays there's just so much noise that I can't help but wonder if kids today get to experience the great outdoors in the same way we did when we were growing up? If not, they should.

I'll admit though that my idea of heaven isn't really everyone's enamel mug of moerkoffie (think soccer moms, girly boys, girly girls and anyone who's scared of the dark, of insects and of owls going 'hoo' in the night). BUT there are so many great reasons you should get in your car and get out there with your family ... especially in South Africa. Our ancestors had the right idea on their ox wagons, and really all we've done is make our 'groot trek' a little easier and a lot more modern. But the silence? The silence is exactly the same.

JAFFLES ON THE BRAAI ARE PROBABLY THE
EASIEST CAMPING FOOD YOU CAN DO AND A
GREAT EXCUSE TO BUTTER BOTH SIDES OF YOUR
BREAD. THIS IS WHAT WE USED BEFORE THE
ARRIVAL OF THE SNACKWICH MACHINE AND WHAT
I STILL USE EVERY HOLIDAY. WHAT YOU DECIDE TO
PUT INSIDE YOUR JAFFLE IS ENTIRELY UP TO YOU,
BUT IF YOU'RE THE KIND OF PERSON WHO ORDERS
THEIR PIZZA WITH EXTRA BANANA ON IT, THEN
THIS JAFFLE IS RIGHT UP YOUR ALLEY.

BANANA AND HAM JAFFLES

BY JACQUES & NADIA

Butter one side of each slice of bread and remember the buttered sides will be on the outside of the jaffles. Spread the minced garlic on the unbuttered centre of one slice of bread. Arrange some Parma ham over the garlic, but not on the corners as they will get cut off. Cover the ham with sliced banana, the banana with rocket, the rocket with slices of Gruyère, and finally sprinkle with as much or as little chilli as you like. Season with salt and cracked black pepper, and place the other slice of bread on top (buttered side up). Repeat this until you've got enough to feed your friends.

Place the sandwich inside a cold jaffle iron, close it up and cut off the edges of the bread sticking out at the sides. If you do this right, you should only lose some of the bread, but none of the filling.

Braai over moderate coals, checking every now and then that it doesn't burn. When the bread is crisp, but still needs a bit of colour, bang it straight onto the coals to get that delicious toasty golden-brown look. Eat it while it's hot!

YOU'LL NEED:

thick slices of government loaf (this is a whole loaf of bread that you buy from your corner kafee which you actually have to slice yourself – imagine!) You need 2 slices per jaffle.

butter, softened

garlic, minced

Parma ham, shredded

a couple of ripe bananas, sliced

rocket leaves

Gruyère cheese, sliced

red chilli, minced

salt and cracked black pepper, to taste

SPEAKING OF BUTTERING YOUR BREAD ON BOTH SIDES, EVER THOUGHT OF MAKING A GIANT BRAAI BROODJIE? NO? WELL BERTUS DID AND, AS USUAL, IT WAS SIMPLE BUT BRILLIANT. YOU CAN CHOOSE WHATEVER FILLING YOU LIKE, BUT DOUBLE OR TRIPLE THE AMOUNT YOU WOULD USUALLY USE FOR ONE. AND DEFINITELY DO IT IN A SANDWICH GRID. THE BRAAI BROODJIE IS PROBABLY ONE OF THE BEST GUILTY PLEASURES AT ANY BRAAI – WHETHER IT'S PART OF THE MAIN MEAL OR A SNACK FOR YOUR FRIENDS WHILE THEY'RE WAITING FOR THE REAL DEAL. AND WHEN YOU MAKE IT BIGGER AND BETTER? IT BECOMES SOMETHING FOR THE BOYTJIES IN A WORLD WHERE SIZE TRULY DOES MATTER.

THE GIANT BRAAI BROODJIE

 BERTUS BASSON

FOR ONE GIANT BRAAI BROODJIE, YOU'LL NEED:

2 thick slices of government loaf, cut lengthways

butter, softened

2–3 handfuls of cheddar cheese, grated

half a small onion, thinly sliced

about 2 big beefy tomatoes, sliced

coarse sea salt and cracked black pepper, to taste

Carefully cut two slices of bread from the loaf – lengthways. Spread each slice of bread generously with butter. Flip one slice over and top with cheese, onion and tomato slices. Season with coarse sea salt and cracked black pepper, and close it up with the second slice of bread. Get a friend to take one side of the braai broodjie; you take the other and move it over to the braai grid, butter on the outsides of the broodjie. Put the grid over moderate coals and slowly toast one side until golden brown and crunchy, then flip it over to toast the other side. It's done perfectly if it's toasty and golden and the cheese oozes out when you bite into it. Now you can either cut it up, or serve one per boytjie ... which is what I suggest you do.

TUCKING INTO A PIE FOR DINNER WHILE YOU'RE WARMING YOUR FEET NEAR THE FIRE IS JUST A LITTLE BIT OF THAT MAGIC YOU CAN EXPERIENCE WHEN YOU'RE CAMPING IN THE GREAT OUTDOORS. AND, WHILE THIS RECIPE LOOKS MIGHTILY IMPRESSIVE AND DIFFICULT TO MAKE, IT'S ACTUALLY AS EASY AS, WELL … AS EASY AS PIE. YOU CAN MAKE TWO VERSIONS OF THIS PIE, BOTH WITH THE SAME FILLING. ONE HAS A PASTRY TOPPING AND THE OTHER IS INDIVIDUAL COTTAGE PIES IN ENAMEL MUGS WITH MASHED ROOT VEGETABLE TOPPINGS. YOU CAN CHOOSE WHICH ONE YOU FEEL LIKE MAKING OR EVEN DO BOTH IF YOU WANT TO MIX IT UP.

VENISON POT PIES

 JUSTIN BONELLO

THE FILLING

Toss the gemsbok in seasoned flour. Heat the butter and a glug of olive oil in a flat-bottomed potjie over moderate coals. Seal the cubed meat, then scoop it out and set aside. In the same potjie pot, fry the bacon, onion, celery, chopped carrots, rosemary, thyme, cumin, coriander, garlic and chilli flakes until fragrant. Next stir in the tomatoes and the tomato paste, fry for a couple of minutes and deglaze with red wine. Add the potatoes, meat, stock, sugar and bay leaves, reduce the heat of the coals and simmer for about three to four hours, or until the venison is nice and tender.

Now, I hate to do this to you, but it's going to make a world of difference. Take a slotted spoon and scoop out the cooked chuck, let it cool down to touching temperature, then shred the meat (it should be soft enough just to pull apart). Put it back into the pot, season with salt and pepper, then stir through the chopped parsley and baby spinach. Because the meat has been shredded, it's going to really mix into the juices and taste so much better.

FOR THE FILLING, YOU'LL NEED:

1 kg gemsbok chuck, diced – if you can't find gemsbok, use any other venison or even free-range beef chuck

about 2 cups of flour, seasoned with salt and cracked black pepper

1 or 2 big knobs of butter

a large glug of olive oil

½ packet of free-range streaky bacon, diced

2 onions, finely chopped

2–3 carrots, peeled and chopped

2–3 celery sticks, chopped

a small handful of chopped rosemary

2 small handfuls of chopped thyme

about 1 tablespoon of ground cumin

2 teaspoons of ground coriander

2 teaspoons of dried chilli flakes

3–4 garlic cloves, crushed and chopped

1 can of whole peeled tomatoes

about 3 tablespoons of tomato paste

a couple of glasses of red wine

4–5 large potatoes, peeled and diced

a couple of pinches of sugar

1 cup of beef stock

2 bay leaves

salt and pepper, to taste

a handful of flat-leaf parsley, chopped

3 big handfuls of baby spinach

VENISON POT PIES

Depending on which pie you've decided to make, do the following:

★ THE PASTRY PIE ★

Gently roll out a sheet of thawed puff pastry so that it's slightly bigger than the potjie you're using, then brush a little egg over the top. Carefully lay the pastry over the opening of the gemsbok pot, pressing down the edges to secure on the side. Brush with more egg, and make a little knife incision in the centre of the pastry. Pop the lid on, place the potjie on a tripod over moderate coals, with a couple of embers placed on top of the lid to create an oven. Bake for about 25 to 30 minutes or until the pastry is deliciously golden.

YOU'LL NEED:
a roll of puff pastry, thawed
1 egg, beaten

★ THE MUG PIES ★

Simmer sweet potato, parsnip, carrot, butternut and potato with garlic and onion in stock until cooked through. Mash with a knob of butter, a dash of cream and a generous handful of grated Parmesan and chopped parsley. Scoop the gemsbok filling into as many enamel cups as you can fill, and spoon the root veg mash over the top. Pour some water into a flat-bottomed potjie and place the enamel cups into the water (the water level should reach about the halfway mark on the cups). Pop the lid on, cover with coals and bake over a moderate heat for about 30 to 40 minutes or until simmering and golden. Eat the pies straight out of the mugs.

YOU'LL NEED:
1 sweet potato, peeled and cubed
2 parsnips, roughly chopped
2 carrots, roughly chopped
about half a butternut, peeled and cubed
1–2 potatoes, cubed
2 garlic cloves, crushed and chopped
1 onion, chopped
2 cups of beef stock
a generous knob of butter
a dash of cream
a big handful of Parmesan, grated
a sprinkling of parsley, chopped

THIS IS A PRETTY NIFTY WAY TO MAKE TORTILLAS WHEN YOU'RE CAMPING. THANKS FOR THE RECIPE, JACQUES! IT'S GENIUS.

ZIPLOCK TORTILLAS

JACQUES & NADIA

Find a comfortable spot around the fire then pour the flour into the ziplock bag, add the butter and rub with your fingertips until crumbly. Dissolve the salt in the water, then pour the salted water into the bag. Close the bag (that's why you need a ziplock) and (in Jacques' words) moer everything around. This, for those of you who don't understand 'big Afrikaner Afrikaans', means mix it by shaking it vigorously (and in a manly way).

Sprinkle some flour onto a clean surface, cut a hole into the bag and squeeze the dough out of the bag onto the surface. Sprinkle more flour over the dough and lightly knead. Cut into eight pieces, sprinkle with flour again, then roll the balls out with a rolling pin to the desired size. Jacques likes his to be thin and dinner-plate size, but it's really up to your own taste.

Heat up a big pan over moderate to hot coals, and dry-fry each individual tortilla. Flip it over once the underside is golden. Repeat until you've finished up all the dough.

FOR EIGHT TORTILLAS, YOU'LL NEED:

2 cups of plain flour

1 large ziplock bag

¼ cup of butter

½ teaspoon of salt

½–¾ cup of water

★ ★ ★ ★ ★

This is great with a SPIT BRAAI (page 46) and different dips and fillings. You could even do these with COWBOY BEANS (page 135) or make it as part of your TAPAS PLATTER (page 160 - 167).

★

THIS IS POSSIBLY THE MOST BRILLIANT CONCEPT I'VE EVER COME ACROSS,
THANKS TO OUR SERIOUSLY GREAT FOOD STYLIST, CARO. IT MAKES ME JUST
WANT TO REPEAT THE WORDS OVER AND OVER AGAIN ... 'WAFFLE JAFFLE
WAFFLE JAFFLE WAFFLE JAFFLE WAFFLE JAFFLE.' I HATE THAT I WASN'T THE
ONE WHO THOUGHT OF THIS ... IT BRINGS A WHOLE NEW LEVEL TO WHAT YOU
CAN DO ON THE BRAAI FOR DESSERT WHEN ALL YOU HAVE IS A JAFFLE IRON,
A FIRE AND, COINCIDENTALLY, THE BASIC INGREDIENTS TO MAKE WAFFLES.
SOOOOO TASTY ... THANKS, CARO.

WAFFLE JAFFLES

 CARO

YOU'LL NEED:

2 cups of cake flour, sifted

1 teaspoon of baking powder

a pinch of salt

1 teaspoon of baking soda

2 eggs, beaten

1½–2 cups of buttermilk

¼ cup of butter, melted

Mix sifted flour, baking powder, salt and baking soda in a large bowl. Add the eggs, buttermilk and butter then mix well (you can just use a wooden spoon or big whisk for this). Grease the jaffle irons with some butter, then place over moderate coals. Once they're hot, ladle waffle batter onto the jaffle irons, close them up and wait for the waffles to be crisp, golden and cooked through. (You'll need to turn them over a couple of times.) Take them out of the jaffles, keep warm on the side and repeat until you've used up all the batter.

 SERVE WITH Chocolate sauce, ice cream and berries (or whatever tickles your fancy) and definitely some really good coffee to wash it all down.

SHOWING PART OF SOUTHERN AFRICA WITH
SOME ROADS AND PLACES AND WITH
BOUNDARIES NATURAL REPLACING NATIONAL

1:2,000,000

WHEN YOU TRAVEL AS OFTEN AS I DO, IT'S NOTHING UNUSUAL TO FIND THE ODDEST LITTLE TOWNS. SOMETIMES I FIND THESE PURELY BECAUSE I SEE A STRANGE NAME THAT I'VE NEVER SEEN BEFORE AND TRAVEL THERE OUT OF PURE CURIOSITY, AND OTHER TIMES MY CREW AND I JUST TAKE THE WRONG TURN (AGAIN). BUT WHEN THIS HAPPENS, MY INNER MODERN-DAY COLUMBUS IS RARELY DISAPPOINTED WITH MY LATEST DISCOVERY.

Wakkerstroom was a bit like one of these discoveries because I knew absolutely nothing about it, except where it was located on the map. I think this little gem (and the second oldest town in southern Mpumalanga) is one of the most hospitable little places I've ever been to – and that includes the hundreds of Karoo towns I've gone to in the past two years. Wakkerstroom forms part of internationally recognised wetlands, so it's famous to twitchers for the great number of birds, who stop off from Europe on their migrations, and the vast number of endemic species found here. Because of the altitude the area experiences warm and sometimes wet summers with spectacular thunderstorms, but on the flipside it means that winters are icy cold and at night temperatures drop below zero, turning green grasslands, which rank with the American prairies and the Russian Steppe, into a vast landscape of muted tones.

I imagine that most people who actually know about Wakkerstroom and travel there every year are South African twitchers hoping to tick off another bird from their lists. But I'm not an avid bird watcher (except in my younger years ... but those were birds of a different feather), so to me this beautiful valley was just a great spot to escape the stimulation and pollution of urban life. And one of the best ways I know how to do that? By raiding the contestants' camp next to the railway station at Ossewakop, lighting a fire and braaiing and eating good steak. At least, that's what we did ...

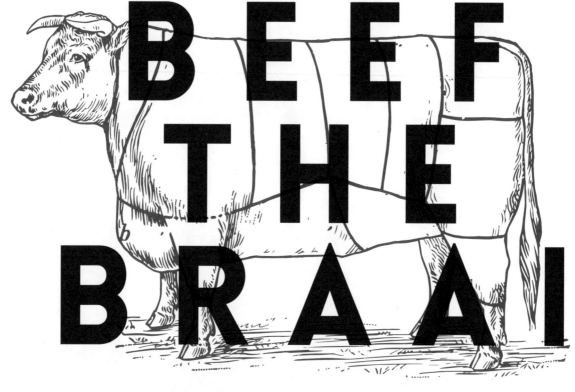

BEEF THE BRAAI

CRAVING A LEKKER BRAAIED STEAK, BUT CONFUSED ABOUT WHICH CUT TO GET? HERE ARE MY TOP FIVE STEAKS FOR THE BRAAI.

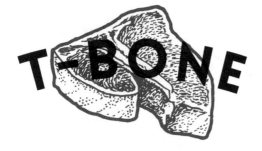

T-BONE

THIS IS THE CLASSIC GO-TO STEAK FOR BIG, BURLY MEN (AND WOMEN) WITH BIG HUNGER. IT'S CUT FROM THE SHORT LOIN AND HAS A T-SHAPED BONE WITH NEW YORK STRIP STEAK ON ONE SIDE AND FILET MIGNON ON THE OTHER. IT'S THE BEST OF BOTH WORLDS.

CUT FROM THE SMALLER END OF THE TENDERLOIN, IT'S THE TENDEREST CUT OF BEEF WITH A BUTTER-LIKE QUALITY. IN FACT, IF YOU DO IT RIGHT, YOU SHOULD BE ABLE TO CUT THROUGH IT WITH A BUTTER KNIFE. THE LADIES LOVE IT.

FILLET

RIB-EYE

THIS STEAK IS CUT FROM THE RIB SECTION AND MANY PEOPLE MIGHT NOT KNOW THIS, BUT IT IS ONE OF THE MORE TASTY AND TENDER CUTS OF BEEF WITH A BUTTERY FLAVOUR BECAUSE OF ALL THE MARBLED FAT. GOOD FOR A SLOW ROAST. BETTER FOR A BRAAI.

CHIMICHURRI IS A SPECIFIC CONCOCTION OF HERBS FROM ARGENTINA AND ONE OF THE BEST ACCOMPANIMENTS FOR STEAK. ADD BUTTER AND YOU HAVE A WINNER! MARTHINUS MAKES THIS RECIPE IN HIS AWARD-WINNING RESTAURANT DW-ELEVEN-13 IN JOZI, BUT IT CAN JUST AS EASILY BE DONE ON THE BRAAI. YOU CAN EITHER BLITZ ALL THE CHIMICHURRI INGREDIENTS TOGETHER IN A BLENDER, OR IF YOU'RE AROUND A FIRE, SIMPLY CHOP EVERYTHING UP FINELY BEFORE MIXING WITH BUTTER.

CHIMICHURRI BUTTER RIB-EYE

 MARTHINUS FERREIRA

YOU'LL NEED:
a small handful of fresh oregano, finely chopped
a small handful of flat-leaf parsley, finely chopped
a small handful of fresh coriander
2 chillies, seeds removed and finely chopped
2 garlic cloves, crushed and chopped
juice of half a lemon and 1 lime
a couple of knobs of butter
a couple of good quality, free-range rib-eye steaks
a glug of olive oil
salt and pepper, to taste

Mix the herbs, chillies, garlic and lemon together in a large bowl, add the butter and mush everything together with a fork. Rub the rib-eye steaks with olive oil and season with salt and pepper. Braai over a moderate to hot fire for a couple of minutes a side.

 SERVE WITH A generous dollop of chimichurri butter on each steak, CHARRED BROCCOLI AND ASPARAGUS (page 19), and HASSLEBACK SPUDS (page 136).

RUMP

WITH IT'S THICK SIDE OF FAT, RUMP IS CONSIDERED TO BE ONE OF THE MORE FLAVOURFUL CUTS OF STEAK. CRISP UP THE FAT BEFORE BRAAIING THE STEAK. BEST SERVED MEDIUM RARE.

One of Cape Town's oldest and most popular hidden gems is a Portuguese restaurant called Dias Tavern, and if you're ever in the Mother City you have to go there. When you walk in you don't expect much because of the décor (plastic chairs and cheap-looking Castle Lager tablecloths), but this is the spot where clever Capetonians go to for a real trinchado, peri-peri chicken or prego roll. Once you've tasted their array of secret sauces, you'll probably spend many nights at home trying to replicate them ... to no avail. And no matter how nicely you ask the owners of Dias, they'll refuse to give their closely guarded recipes away.

The last place in the world I expected to find something even remotely close to Dias's famous trinchado was in the small town of Wakkerstroom. But when you're good friends with one of South Africa's top ten chefs and he decides to do his take on this traditional Portuguese dish, you can't really be surprised. And the best part of all? He's willing to share his recipe with you. It's not the exact same taste, but I dare say that Bertus's trinchado might actually be better. And the bonus? You can make it on the braai anywhere in the great outdoors. Here we go.

★ REAL TRINCHADO ★

 BERTUS BASSON

Start by cutting the rump steak into big cubes then put a fireproof pan over hot coals. Add a splash of oil and once hot, pop in the cubes of meat. Seal the rump on all sides – this shouldn't take longer than a couple of minutes – then add the garlic, chilli, bay leaves and thyme, and fry for a couple of seconds. Add the port and once it has reduced, add the beef stock, cream, olives and fresh parsley. Remove from the heat immediately so that the meat is still medium rare and soft, season with salt and pepper and tuck in! Don't boil the meat – you'll end up eating meat resembling dry, cubed cardboard.

This is my kind of recipe because it doesn't require any fancy plating ... eat it straight from the pan, using a fork for the meat and the bread rolls to mop up that lekker spicy sauce. So good!

FOR TWO PEOPLE, YOU'LL NEED:

about 500 g good quality, free-range rump steak, fat removed and cut into big chunks

olive oil

about 3 garlic cloves, crushed and sliced

about 2 chillies, seeds removed and finely chopped

2 bay leaves

3 sprigs of thyme

1 shot of port

1 cup of beef stock

2 splashes of cream

about 15 Kalamata olives, pits removed

a small handful of chopped fresh parsley

salt and pepper, to taste

fresh Portuguese rolls

SIRLOIN

THIS IS ONE OF MY FAVOURITES, CUT FROM THE REAR BACK PORTION OF THE COW OR BULL, NEAR THE RUMP. DON'T OVERCOOK OTHERWISE YOU'LL END UP WITH CHEWY, FLAVOURLESS STEAK. DONE BEST QUICKLY OVER A HIGH HEAT.

IN THE BATTLE FOR THE PERFECT STEAK, YOU CAN'T DO MUCH WRONG WITH A GOOD OLD BISTRO-STYLE STEAK AND PEPPERCORN SAUCE. WHILE BERTUS LOVES HIS TRINCHADO, AND MARTHINUS SWEARS HIS CHIMICHURRI RIB-EYE IS THE WINNER, I THINK WE ALL KNOW THAT IF YOU KEEP THE INGREDIENTS SIMPLE AND USE A GOOD CUT OF MEAT, YOU'RE BOUND TO BE HAPPY WITH THE RESULT. I UNOFFICIALLY (OFFICIALLY) DECLARE MYSELF THE WINNER OF THE PERFECT STEAK. YOU'RE WELCOME.

FLAME-BRAAIED ★ STEAK ★

 JUSTIN BONELLO

FOR THE PEPPERCORN SAUCE, YOU'LL NEED:

a big knob of unsalted butter

1 onion, finely chopped

4–5 sprigs of thyme, finely chopped

2–3 garlic cloves

about 2–3 tablespoons of green peppercorns (the bottled kind), half of them crushed and the rest kept whole

a decent splash of brandy

just under 1 cup of good beef stock

about 1 cup of cream

salt and pepper, to taste

FOR THE PERFECT STEAK, YOU'LL NEED:

steak rub (page 108)

1 steak per person – any cut you like (I used sirloin)

sunflower oil

Melt the butter in a fireproof pan over moderate coals then add the chopped onion, thyme and garlic, and sauté until softened. Next add all the peppercorns and stir. Pour in a splash of brandy and flambé – do this by either tipping the pan into the fire, or by using a lighter – but be careful not to burn your hands ... or eyebrows! Let the flame die a natural death to allow the alcohol to cook off, then add the beef stock and cream. Simmer for about 30 minutes on a low heat or until the sauce has reduced by half. Season with salt and pepper.

Just before the sauce is ready (say about ten minutes), it's time to braai the steak. I used thick-cut sirloin steaks, but use whatever steak is your favourite. Make sure the coals are nice and hot, then after you've generously rubbed the steaks with the spices, seal them on the fire. Once the steaks are sealed on both sides, drizzle with sunflower oil and let the flames lick (not burn) the one side. Turn the steak around and do the same on the other side. The taste this creates is worth the fire hazard you're causing, trust me. Remove the sealed steaks from the heat, let them rest then, once your peppercorn sauce is just about ready, cut the sirloin into friend-size portions and braai to your friends' tastes (rare, medium rare or medium – I think anything more than that is sacrilege). Drizzle with peppercorn sauce and tuck in. Lekker ...

OLD-SCHOOL STEAKS

Yep, fasten your seatbelts, folks! We're taking another trip back into the 70s. There's something great about reviving old classic dishes and giving them a new twist. The twist here is that you're going to make it on the braai and impress the hell out of your friends. These recipes are quite long, so I'll just get on with it.

THIS BEAUTY HAS NOTHING TO DO WITH THE LATE GREAT PRINCESS, BUT THE NAME ACTUALLY HAS ITS ROOTS IN THE ROMAN GODDESS OF THE HUNT (SEEMS FITTING, DOESN'T IT?). BACK IN THE DAY WHEN LIFE SEEMED A LITTLE SLOWER, IT USED TO BE SERVED AS AN ENTRÉE IN SOME VERY LARNEY RESTAURANTS – FLAMBÉED AT YOUR TABLE. IT'S A ONE-PAN RECIPE, AND TAKES VERY LITTLE TIME TO MAKE, SO THERE'S NO REASON YOU SHOULDN'T TRY IT AT HOME!

STEAK DIANE

BY JUSTIN BONELLO

FOR TWO PEOPLE, YOU'LL NEED:

about 2 tablespoons of butter

2 x 175 g filet mignons (French for 'dainty fillet'), seasoned with salt and pepper

1 medium-sized onion, finely diced

about a handful of button mushrooms, sliced

about 2 teaspoons of Dijon mustard

a couple of tablespoons of Worcester sauce

⅓ cup of red wine

about 80 ml beef stock

a splash of brandy

about 1 cup of cream

a small handful of fresh flat-leaf parsley, chopped

salt and freshly ground black pepper, to taste

BRAAI IT

Heat half the butter in a large frying pan over hot coals and fry the fillets for a minute on each side. Take the steaks out and set aside, then in the same pan add more butter, reduce the heat of the coals, and fry the chopped onions and mushrooms. Once the onions have softened, add the mustard and Worcester sauce, stirring well. Pour in the red wine and beef stock, and simmer until the sauce is reduced by about a third, then add the brandy and (carefully) flambé the sauce until the flames die a natural death. (Yes, if you want to you can run to the table your friends are sitting at and do it there – it's always a crowd pleaser.) Stir through the cream and simmer for another three minutes or until the sauce has thickened and reduced again. Stir in the parsley, salt and cracked black pepper, then add the steaks. Once they've warmed through, take them off the braai. Get ready to eat some of the most deliciously tender steak you've ever had the honour of putting in your mouth!

THE IDEA OF STUFFING A STEAK WITH OYSTERS MIGHT SOUND BIZARRE TO SOME OF YOU … PERHAPS EVEN GLUTTONOUS, BUT WHEN YOU TASTE IT, YOU'LL UNDERSTAND. YOU GET THE BEST OF TWO SERIOUSLY GREAT WORLDS: THE FRESH TASTE OF THE SEA IN THE STUFFING AND THAT LEKKER UMAMI YOU CAN ONLY EVER GET WHEN YOU BRAAI MEAT OVER THE OPEN FIRE. THERE ARE LOADS OF VARIATIONS OF THIS CLASSIC STEAK, AND THIS IS MINE …

CARPETBAGGER

 BY JUSTIN BONELLO

YOU'LL NEED:

3 big knobs of butter

about 8 oysters, shucked – make sure you've removed any shell fragments

a couple of splashes of Tabasco

zest of 1 lemon

salt and cracked black pepper, to taste

about a handful of fresh breadcrumbs

1 fillet – any size will do, but if it's bigger than about 600 g, increase the quantities of your ingredients

a big handful of chopped chives

a squeeze of lemon juice

toothpicks

THE STUFFING

Place a fireproof pan over moderate coals and melt the butter. Chuck in the oysters and stir in the Tabasco (to your own taste), the lemon zest, salt and black pepper. Fry for about a minute, until the oysters have firmed up slightly, then take them off the heat, put everything in a mixing bowl and sprinkle in the breadcrumbs. Stir in enough crumbs to suck up and absorb all the juices and let it cool down to touching temperature. Take the fillet and cut a deep pocket into the meat, lengthways. Stop cutting about 2 cm from the bottom. Using a tablespoon (or your hands), stuff the crumbed oysters into the pocket, but be careful that you don't overstuff the fillet otherwise the stuffing will spill out when you braai it. Take as many toothpicks as you need to close the pocket up and skewer them through the fillet to close the opening. Rub salt and pepper onto the fillet and place on a grill over moderate to hot coals. Braai for about five minutes a side, turning the fillet only once.

 SERVE

Medium rare and garnish with a couple of chopped chives and a squeeze of lemon juice.

★

EVEN THOUGH THIS ENGLISH FAVOURITE IS USUALLY DONE IN AN OVEN, YOU CAN (ALMOST) JUST AS EASILY DO IT ON THE BRAAI. IT'S A LOT OF WORK (BUT TOTALLY WORTH IT!) SO LURE YOUR FRIENDS WITH SOME BEERS AND GET THEM TO HELP. OUR MOTTO (AND SOMETIMES CHALLENGE) ON THE ROAD IS THAT ANYTHING YOU CAN DO IN THE KITCHEN, WE CAN DO ON THE FIRE. IF YOU'RE AN EXPAT LIVING IN LONDON, YOU *HAVE* TO TRY THIS!

BEEF WELLINGTON

 JUSTIN BONELLO

★ THE DUXELLES (FANCY FRENCH WORD FOR MUSHROOM PASTE VIBES)

YOU'LL NEED:

2 knobs of butter, softened

a small glug of canola oil

half an onion, finely chopped

1 punnet of portobello mushrooms, finely chopped and stems removed

about ½ cup of cream

Maldon salt and cracked black pepper, to taste

about 2 big pinches of flat-leaf parsley, finely chopped

Gently heat the butter and oil in a fireproof pan over moderate coals. Stir in the onion and cook until soft, then add the mushrooms. Increase the heat of the coals and add the cream and salt and pepper. Stir vigorously then leave to cook, stirring occasionally until the cream has reduced and the mushrooms are cooked. This should take about 15 minutes and should be quite dry. Take it off the heat, mix in the chopped parsley and set aside. While you're making the duxelles, get a friend you trust to make the crêpes.

★ THE CRÊPES

YOU'LL NEED:

½ cup of flour

a pinch of salt

2 eggs

¾ cup of milk – add more if the batter is too thick

4 knobs of butter

In a large bowl, sieve together the flour and salt. Make a well in the centre, crack in the two eggs and add a splash of milk. Using a wooden spoon, start mixing and once it starts resembling a thick batter, take a whisk and gradually whisk in the remaining milk, a little bit at a time, until you have a smooth batter.

Take a large non-stick fireproof pan and place it over medium to hot coals and melt a knob of butter. Swirl the pan around to grease it evenly, then give it a quick wipe with a paper towel. Ladle in enough batter to cover the entire pan – swirl the pan again to ensure the batter coats the entire base. Cook for about a minute on one side, then flip the crêpe over and cook the other side for about 30 seconds or until done. Repeat this until you have four crêpes – if you have any leftover batter (and energy) make the rest of the crêpes, sprinkle with cinnamon sugar and give them to your friends as a snack.

⭐ ALL THE REST…

YOU'LL NEED:

about 1 kg free-range fillet

salt and pepper, to taste

a splash of canola oil

just under 1 cup of chicken liver pâté

1 roll of puff pastry, thawed but kept cool

½ cup of flour

1 egg, whisked

a knob of unsalted butter, melted

1 roll of thawed puff pastry, rolled out
and cut into two sheets

Pat the beef dry, give it a good rubbing with salt and black pepper, then place the beef in a bit of oil in a pan over a high heat. Sear until it is browned all over – about two to three minutes on each side. Take the beef out of the pan and set aside to cool down. While the beef is cooling, mash the chicken liver pâté and the duxelles together until you have something resembling a soft paste.

Carefully place the four crêpes on a clean working surface, overlapping them just enough to make a rough square shape. Scoop the mushroom and liver paste over the crêpes and spread it out evenly. Take the now-cooled beef and pop it into the centre of the crêpes. Carefully wrap the crêpes around the fillet, tucking them underneath the beef (like you would tuck in a sleeping child). Trim off any excess crêpe at the ends.

Fuse two sheets of puff pastry together (do this by overlapping the two edges and then sticking them together by flattening the edges with a rolling pin). Next, lightly flour a clean surface and roll out the puff pastry into a rectangle. Pop the wrapped beef on top of the pastry, tucking back any of the crêpe that's come loose in the process. Fold the pastry up and around the beef, smoothing out any pockets of air as you go. Brush some egg along the bottom edge of the seam and then press down gently to seal it. Do this right around the Wellington until it's completely sealed. Trim off any excess pastry.

Carefully lift the Wellington onto a greased baking sheet and refrigerate for about 30 minutes. Take it out of the fridge and brush it with melted butter to glaze. Take a sharp knife and lightly score the top of the pastry, but be careful not to cut all the way through. Put the Wellington onto a rack and into a kassie, then bake over moderate coals until golden brown. Take it out and let it rest on a wooden board for ten minutes before cutting thick slices to serve.

CHATEAUBRIAND IS A FANCY WORD FOR A CUT FROM THE THICKEST PART OF THE TENDERLOIN, BUT WE JUST CALL IT FILLET ... WE'RE NOT UP OUR OWN ... WELL, YOU KNOW. I PROMISE YOU THE NAME OF THIS CLASSIC FRENCH STEAK IS A LOT HARDER TO PRONOUNCE THAN IT IS TO ACTUALLY MAKE IT! ALSO, ANNOUNCE TO YOUR FRIENDS LOUDLY (AND WITH YOUR NOSE SLIGHTLY POINTED TOWARDS THE HEAVENS) THAT YOU'LL BE BRAAIING A 'SHA-TOE-BREE-AAAHN' (WITH THE TYPICAL MY-NOSE-IS-BLOCKED N AT THE END) AND THEY'LL BE IMPRESSED WITHOUT EVEN TASTING IT YET!

CHATEAUBRIAND WITH BÉARNAISE SAUCE

 JUSTIN BONELLO

First up you're going to make the Béarnaise sauce by putting the white wine, vinegar, peppercorns and chopped onion in a fireproof saucepan and slowly bring it up to the boil. (The wine and vinegar cut through the creaminess of the sauce.) Reduce the heat and simmer the sauce until it's reduced by about half then using a slotted spoon, remove the peppercorns and pour the sauce into a bowl. Next, separate the eggs and whisk the egg yolks until they're stiff, then add the lemon juice and place the bowl over a pan of simmering water (bain-marie). Whisk it all together until it's thicker. While you're whisking away, get a friend to melt some butter and hand it to you so that you can gradually (and constantly) whisk it into the thickened egg yolk. (Think about this process as similar to when you add oil to egg when making mayonnaise.) Take the sauce off the heat, stir in the dried tarragon and salt and black pepper to taste. You can also add a bit of chopped parsley like I do, but that's totally up to you.

Put the Béarnaise sauce to the side and braai your fillet while basting it with melted butter every time you turn it. It should take about 20 minutes to get the fillet to medium rare, depending on how big the cut of meat is. Once done to your liking, let the meat rest for about five minutes before cutting it into thick slices. Serve with a generous dollop of the Béarnaise sauce.

⭐ THE BÉARNAISE SAUCE

YOU'LL NEED:

about 50 ml white wine

a dash of tarragon vinegar

about 1 teaspoon of dried white peppercorns – if you can't find these, use a teaspoon of green peppercorns (the ones you get in jars)

1 small onion, finely diced

4 egg yolks

juice of a wedge of lemon

about 4 knobs of butter, melted

salt and cracked black pepper, to taste

a small handful of dried tarragon

a small handful of parsley, chopped (optional)

⭐ THE CHATEAUBRIAND

YOU'LL NEED:

about 600–800 g thick-cut free-range fillet

a big knob of butter

RUBS

Sometimes when you have a really great piece of meat or an almost-swimming-it's-so-fresh piece of fish, you don't need much seasoning and flavour other than a little salt and pepper. But there are other times when meat or fish screams for a little extra loving, in the shape of a great rub lovingly massaged into the flesh. It's a great way to add more flavour, but you should also know when to use a dry rub and when to wet it up.

A dry rub is pretty much just that – a different mixture of spices and herbs that, when you do it right, forms a crust around the meat. Use this when you're braaiing something that cooks fast on high temperatures and when you want something that's going to burst with flavour on the outside without affecting the quality of the taste you expect on the inside. There are no real rules in this space: use your instinct and sense of smell – the combination of herbs and spices you smell will give you a good idea of what it will taste like. The best thing about a dry rub is that, once you've discovered a really great one, you can store it in an airtight container for months and use it over and over again.

A wet rub is a little more exotic and more often than not it's oil based (You can also use beer, soy sauce, water, honey and so on.) It's pretty simple – add some moisture to a dry rub and there you go. Wet rub done. This is used best when rubbed into the meat generously for slow cooking – think ribs, pork chops and any type of chicken. The only tip I can give you here is that when you use oil in a wet rub, it's a great way to draw out those lekker flavours in fresh herbs.

Whether you use a wet or a dry rub there is one secret for both: rub the meat generously and let it sleep in the rub for at least 30 minutes before cooking.

Here are a few of my favourite combinations.

STEAK RUB

Roughly bash together equal quantities of:

coriander
garlic
mustard seeds
rainbow peppercorns
Maldon salt

VENISON RUB

This is enough for one springbok loin (page 19).
If the piece of venison is bigger, make more.

200 g Maldon salt
50 g ground coriander
40 g white sugar
4 or 5 sprigs of fresh thyme
2 garlic cloves, crushed
5 g paprika

CHICKEN RUB

Nice for a lekker spicy, zesty
chicken braai.

zest of one lemon
equal quantities of:
paprika; cumin seeds; treacle
sugar; chilli flakes; Maldon salt;
black pepper; dried thyme

FISH RUB

Great for any kind of seafood, but
especially whole fish.

juice of 1 lime
about 2 tablespoons of coconut oil
a handful of basil, chopped
1 stalk of lemon grass, bruised and chopped
2 tablespoons of brown sugar
a handful of mint, chopped
a handful of coriander, chopped
2 garlic cloves, crushed
and chopped
2 chillies, seeds removed and chopped
a chunk of ginger, grated
about 1 teaspoon of Maldon salt
about 1 teaspoon of cracked black pepper

GARLIC RUB

Good on anything ...

2 handfuls of parsley,
finely chopped
about 1 tablespoon of
rosemary, finely chopped
8–10 large garlic cloves,
crushed and roughly chopped
a couple of glugs of olive oil
a couple of pinches of
cracked black pepper
a pinch of salt
1 chilli, chopped
a big pinch of brown sugar
a big pinch of ground cumin

ORIENTAL DIPPING SAUCE

Put all the ingredients (except the fresh herbs) into a pot and bring to the boil. Once the sugar has dissolved, take it off the heat and let it cool down. Finally, add the fresh herbs and mix it all together. Serve with oriental chicken (page 30).

YOU'LL NEED:

juice of 1 lime and 1 lemon

50 ml fish sauce

a splash of water

a big glug of Kikkoman soy sauce

50 g treacle sugar

1 chilli, chopped

1 garlic clove, crushed and chopped

a chunk of ginger, chopped

a handful of both fresh coriander and basil, chopped

SAUCY STUFF

JANET'S FISH SAUCE

Heat up a splash of canola and sesame seed oil in a saucepan. Quickly fry the garlic, ginger, chilli and fennel seeds (about 30 seconds) then squeeze in the tamarind pulp through your hands so just the juice goes into the pan. Add in the sugar, fish sauce, soy sauce, lemon juice and stir until the sugar has dissolved. Add salt and pepper to taste. Set aside, but keep warm.

Braai your fish, and once the fish is done to perfection, put it in a large serving dish and drizzle generously with the sauce. Finish it off with a generous scattering of chopped mint, basil and coriander.

YOU'LL NEED:

a splash of both canola and sesame seed oil

3–4 garlic cloves, crushed and chopped

1 large chunk of ginger, grated

2 chillies, chopped

about 1 tablespoon of fennel seeds, toasted and ground (optional)

3 tablespoons of tamarind pulp, mixed into ½ cup of water

a big pinch of sugar

about 2–3 tablespoons of fish sauce, to your own taste

a decent splash of Kikkoman soy sauce

juice of 2 lemons

Maldon salt and cracked black pepper, to taste

a handful of mint, chopped

a handful of basil, chopped

a handful of fresh coriander, chopped

⭐ BBQ SAUCE

Use this as a marinade and basting sauce for ribs, chicken and burgers. And keep a jar of it in your fridge. Okay? Good.

Mix all the ingredients together and simmer very gently in a pan for about 30 minutes.

YOU'LL NEED:

about 2½ cups of tomato sauce

4 tablespoons of brown or treacle sugar

a couple of generous splashes of both Kikkoman soy sauce and Worcester sauce

about 3 tablespoons of white spirit vinegar

about 3 tablespoons of Dijon mustard

a dash of cayenne pepper

⭐ MARTHINUS'S KICK-ASS PERI-PERI SAUCE

This sauce has a serious bite, but it's a nice one.

Place the two red peppers over hot coals, turning frequently until chargrilled on all sides. While they're still hot, place them in a bowl, cover with cling wrap and leave to sweat. You'll notice that the skin will start to warp, and once it does, take it out, peel the skin off and chop up the flesh. Put the chopped red pepper, chilli, garlic, thyme, salt and black pepper together, add a pinch of sugar and bash it all up. Scrape the sauce into a larger mixing bowl then stir through a couple of glugs of olive oil and the lemon juice.

Marinate a spatchcocked chicken (page 26) in the sauce overnight or simply bottle it and keep it in your fridge as your go-to peri-peri sauce.

YOU'LL NEED:

2 red peppers

10 chillies, finely chopped – with seeds

5 garlic cloves, crushed and chopped

3–4 sprigs of thyme

salt and black pepper

a pinch of sugar

a couple of glugs of olive oil

juice of 1½ lemons

THIS IS LIKE A TRADITIONAL CAESAR SALAD ... JUST WAAAAY BETTER. EVEN SALAD HATERS WILL LOVE IT, BECAUSE IT'S GOT BACON IN IT. AND WE ALL KNOW EVERYTHING IN LIFE IS JUST SO MUCH BETTER WHEN YOU'VE GOT BACON.

THE ONE-MEAL SALAD

 BERTUS BASSON

FOR THE DRESSING, YOU'LL NEED:

about 3 tablespoons of mayonnaise

about 3 tablespoons of smooth cream cheese

a handful of Parmesan, finely grated

a good squeeze of lemon

a pinch of coarse sea salt and cracked black pepper

FOR ONE MAN-SIZED SALAD, YOU'LL NEED:

4 or 5 rashers of bacon

1 slice of government loaf, cut lengthways, lightly brushed with olive oil

a couple of leaves of cos lettuce

about 5 anchovy fillets

about 5 caper berries

a small handful of Parmesan shavings

juice of 1 lemon

First up, make the fire, and while you're waiting for the coals to be ready, whisk together the salad dressing. Make sure to taste it to check it's got the right amount of seasoning. Once your coals are hot, place the bacon directly on top of the braai grid. Keep a close eye on it, and turn the rashers every so often, until crispy, then take the bacon off. While the bacon's sizzling away, take the slice of bread and pop it onto the same grid. Once it's toasted on the one side, turn it over to crisp up the other side then move it off the heat and onto a plate when it's nice and toasty. Next take the cos lettuce and toss it in the dressing you made earlier. When all the leaves are covered, put it on top of the giant crouton, then scatter the crispy bacon, anchovies, caper berries and Parmesan shavings over the whole lot. Squeeze over some lemon juice, drizzle with the remaining Parmesan dressing and season with coarse sea salt and cracked black pepper. Eat immediately.

DON'T CONFUSE THIS WITH STORE-BOUGHT PASTA YOU GET AT A DELI! YOU'RE GOING TO MAKE THE PESTO CREAM CHEESE YOURSELF, AND I PROMISE YOU, EVERY BITE WILL BE WORTH THE EFFORT! THIS SALAD HAS ALL THE RIGHT COMBINATIONS OF ZESTY, TANGY, CRUNCHY, SALTY AND SPICY, AND WILL DEFINITELY BE A TOP HIT AT ANY BRAAI.

HERBY CREAM CHEESE AND PISTACHIO PASTA SALAD

 JUSTIN BONELLO

YOU'LL NEED:

500 g bag of macaroni or penne

2 giant handfuls of rocket

a giant handful of basil

a big handful of Parmesan, grated

juice and zest of 1 lemon

1 garlic clove, crushed

½ tub of cream cheese

a generous glug of olive oil

salt and cracked black pepper, to taste

a handful of pistachio nuts, peeled and toasted

about 3 big pinches of dried chilli flakes

a packet of free-range streaky bacon, chopped

about 2 cups of cherry tomatoes

Bring a large pot of water to boil, add some salt and olive oil, and cook the pasta until al dente (no longer than ten minutes). While the pasta is cooking, put one handful of rocket, the basil, Parmesan, lemon juice, lemon zest and garlic in a blender and blitz until smooth. Add the cream cheese and olive oil, and mix again until you have a thick herby cream cheese. Season with salt and cracked black pepper, and set aside. By now the pasta should be cooked, so take it off the heat, drain it (reserving a little bit of the water) and set aside to cool down. Heat a non-stick pan and toast the pistachios then set aside. In the same pan, fry the chilli flakes and chopped bacon until crisp, toss in the cherry tomatoes and set aside. Stir a splash of the reserved water through the herby cream cheese. Add the cream cheese to the pasta, along with a little extra lemon juice and a decent glug of olive oil, and stir to loosen the pasta shells from each other. Lastly, toss through the bacon, cherry tomatoes, pistachio nuts and the last handful of rocket before serving.

PORK CHOPS HAVE NEVER BEEN A 'BIG THING' IN SOUTH AFRICA – IN FACT, IF YOU HAD TO ARRIVE AT A BRAAI WITH A PACKET OF PORK CHOPS, YOU'D PROBABLY BE SMIRKED AT OR SHUNNED (EVEN THOUGH THE 'SMIRKERS' OR 'SHUNNERS' WOULD STILL DUTIFULLY BRAAI YOUR CHOPS). I'M NOT ENTIRELY SURE WHY THIS CUT OF PORK HAS SUCH A BAD REP, BUT I THINK IT MIGHT HAVE SOMETHING TO DO WITH ITS TASTY COUSIN, THE LAMB CHOP. MORE THAN THAT, I SUSPECT NONE OF US ACTUALLY KNOW HOW TO BRAAI A PORK CHOP WITHOUT SERVING UP A DRY AND TASTELESS BURNT OFFERING. SO, IN AN ATTEMPT TO REVIVE THIS DELICIOUS PIECE OF MEAT, HERE'S A GREAT LITTLE RECIPE FOR THE PERFECT PORK CHOP. THIS IS MY DOP'S (DIRECTOR OF PHOTOGRAPHY'S) RECIPE, AND I HAVE TO ADMIT, IT'S PRETTY DARN TASTY ...

SOY AND HONEY PORK CHOPS

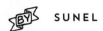 SUNEL

THREE SECRETS TO A GOOD PORK CHOP
One, the thicker the chop, the slower the heat should be; two, use a good marinade or brine; and three, don't try to kill it on the braai – it's already dead.

Mix everything together in a large bowl. Plonk the chops inside the marinade and leave them in the fridge for an hour or two. Just before the fire is ready, remove the chops from the marinade and generously rub salt onto the fat. Now, place the chops (like soldiers) fat side down on the braai to crisp them up (think crackling). Once the fat is nice and crispy (and not burnt) place the chops flesh side down and braai for about seven minutes or until medium, turning frequently and basting with the leftover marinade. When you cut it open, the chop should still be pink inside, but not bloody.

YOU'LL NEED:

a big chunk of ginger, grated

a big splash of sweet soy sauce

½ cup of Kikkoman soy sauce

½ cup of Kikkoman teriyaki sauce

about 2 tablespoons of honey

2 free-range pork chops per friend, at least 3 cm thick

a handful of salt

Hot off the coals with PASTA SALAD (page 113), or PAP AND CHAKALAKA (page 42-43).

PS: This marinade is *great* for duck too!

⭐

AS I'VE SAID BEFORE, VENISON IS A TRICKY THING TO GET RIGHT AND DO WELL, BUT THIS RECIPE IS ONE OF THE BEST I'VE EVER TASTED. FOLLOW IT DOWN TO A T, AND YOU'RE BOUND TO GET IT RIGHT AND BECOME KNOWN AS THE 'VENISON EXPERT' IN YOUR FAMILY … EVEN IF THIS IS THE ONLY VENISON RECIPE YOU EVER MAKE.

BUSH PIG LOIN WITH CHARRED RED PEPPER RELISH

 KATE & JONNO

Place the red peppers directly on the coals until black and charred. While the peppers are on the braai, blanch and dice the tomatoes (remove the skins and seeds). It takes a little effort but is well worth it. Next, take a fireproof pan, add all the seeds (no, not the tomato seeds, stupid) and toast them (tossing them around every now and then to prevent burning). Once they've released their aroma, pop them in a mortar and pestle and bash away. Add the herbs, garlic, red chilli, ginger and lemon zest, and bash it some more. The idea is to get something that resembles a purée texture, so add some olive oil and lemon juice to wet the mixture if it doesn't want to behave. Decant into a mixing bowl and stir in the rest of the olive oil and lemon juice. Season to taste with salt and pepper. Pour half of the mixture over the meat, cover with cling wrap and leave it for about three hours.

YOU'LL NEED:

3 large red peppers

3 large beefy tomatoes, blanched and diced

1 teaspoon of fennel seeds

2 teaspoons of cumin seeds

2 teaspoons of coriander seeds

a giant handful of coriander

a giant handful of Italian parsley

6 garlic cloves, peeled and crushed

3 red chillies, seeds removed and chopped

2 chunks of ginger, sliced

zest of 2 lemons

2 cups of olive oil

⅔ cup of lemon juice, freshly squeezed

1 kg loin of bush pig / venison

about 4 tablespoons of brown sugar

salt and black pepper, to taste

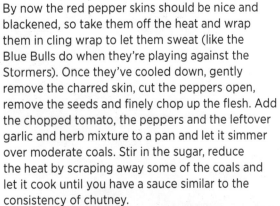

By now the red pepper skins should be nice and blackened, so take them off the heat and wrap them in cling wrap to let them sweat (like the Blue Bulls do when they're playing against the Stormers). Once they've cooled down, gently remove the charred skin, cut the peppers open, remove the seeds and finely chop up the flesh. Add the chopped tomato, the peppers and the leftover garlic and herb mixture to a pan and let it simmer over moderate coals. Stir in the sugar, reduce the heat by scraping away some of the coals and let it cook until you have a sauce similar to the consistency of chutney.

Chuck more wood onto your fire to increase the heat of your coals, and when it's really hot, braai the loin until medium rare. *Don't* overcook the loin – it will taste like cardboard. Take it off the heat, let it rest for five minutes then carve the meat into thin slices and spoon over generous amounts of the pepper relish.

BREAD AND BUTTER PUDDING

 NONO & LEBO

A long time ago (okay, not really THAT long in the greater scheme of things), there were humans on the planet who actually didn't waste food. It wasn't because they were conscious save-the-planet hippies or because they were told not to, but because there was pretty much no food to waste. If you look at the origin of bread and butter pudding, it goes back to the 17th century. And if you look at the 17th century (in general) it really wasn't the best time for most people. (Except for Isaac Newton who discovered calculus, the theory of light, the theory of gravity and the laws of motion ... that guy rocked!) But most other ordinary people were just happy to survive, so when they were lucky enough to have some bread in their homes, even stale bread, they quickly made a plan. And this plan was just the humble beginning of what would become known as the bread and butter pudding ... although, let's face it, it probably didn't have any butter in it. In fact, they added whatever concoction they could get their hands on – from fruit to meat. But as time passed and people became a little more civilised (mostly) and inventive (kind of), they started adding milk and spices, and by the time this recipe reached the middle class it had become a luxury pudding with eggs, milk, butter and sugar. Then one day this classic dessert died a horrible death overnight, only to be revived decades later by the famous foodies we love to hate today. They re-invented it, much like Lebo and Nono did with their version on a VERY cold winter's day in Wakkerstroom. This is comfort food at its best. Enjoy.

⭐ THE SAUCE

YOU'LL NEED:
3 cups of rhubarb, cleaned and chopped
2 cups of white wine
1 cup of brown sugar
2 vanilla pods, seeds scraped out

Put all the ingredients in a flat-bottomed potjie over moderate coals and simmer until the wine has reduced by half and the rhubarb is soft.

⭐ THE PUDDING

YOU'LL NEED:
2 stale French loaves or any white bread you like
1 cup of butter
1 cup of honey
200 g redcurrants

Cut the French loaves into thick slices, then generously spread butter and honey onto two slices at a time and sandwich them together. Do this until you've used up all the bread. Next, cut the sandwiches in half and pack them on top of the rhubarb sauce. Sprinkle with the redcurrants.

⭐ THE CUSTARD

YOU'LL NEED:
1 litre of milk
2 vanilla pods, scraped
12 egg yolks, whisked
1 cup of cream
300 ml sugar
2 cups of raspberries
1 cup of almonds, toasted

In a potjie, pour in the milk and the vanilla, and bring to a gentle simmer. While that's heating up, whisk together the eggs, cream and sugar in a mixing bowl. Pour the warmed milk into the creamed eggs and sugar, and keep stirring until it has combined then pour the custard back into the potjie over a very low heat. Keep stirring until the custard has thickened – you'll need a bit of patience here, but it'll all come together.

Once you have deliciously creamy custard, take it off the heat, then pour it over the bread and rhubarb, and sprinkle generously with the raspberries and toasted almonds. Pop the lid on the potjie and cover with a couple of coals, then place the potjie on a tripod over moderate coals and bake for 30 minutes or until done.

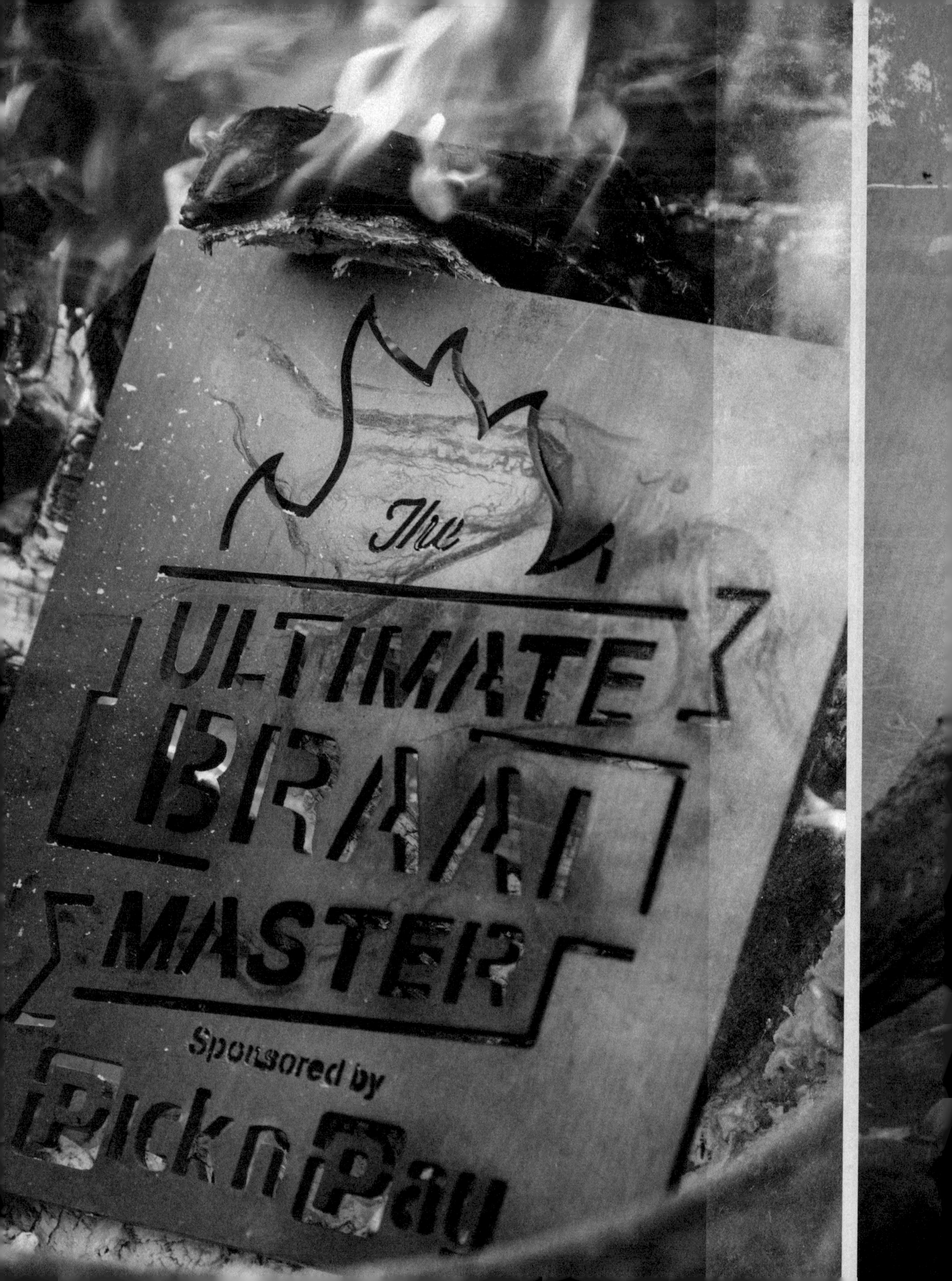
The
ULTIMATE
BRAAI
MASTER
Sponsored by
Pick n Pay

VILLIERSDORP, KNOWN AS THE PEARL OF THE OVERBERG, MIGHT SEEM LIKE
A STRANGE ONE-HORSE TOWN TO GO TO, BUT I HAD A GOOD REASON. ABOUT
3 KM OUTSIDE VILLIERSDORP IS THE APHRODISIAC SHACK – A TRADITIONAL
SMOKEHOUSE ON THE BANKS OF THE THEEWATERSKLOOF DAM. AND THIS IS
WHERE WE FOUND SEAN HORMANN – A CLOSE FRIEND OF BERTUS AND A SMOKER
EXTRAORDINAIRE. AFTER YEARS AND YEARS OF MASTERING THE ART OF HOT
AND COLD SMOKING, I DON'T THINK THERE'S AN INGREDIENT HE HASN'T TRIED
TO SMOKE. CHEESE. BUTTER. HONEY. PEACHES. CHOCOLATE. OIL. SALT. TROUT.
PICKLED ONIONS. OLIVES. YOU NAME IT AND SEAN'S PROBABLY SMOKED IT. SO
WHAT BETTER PLACE TO GO TO SEE A MASTER AT WORK?

THANKS FOR OPENING THE DOORS OF YOUR SMOKEHOUSE
AND YOUR HOME TO US, SEAN!

S M O K E H O U S E

For those of you who aren't lucky enough to own your own smokehouse, but love the taste of smoked food, here are the basics of what you can achieve at home. Just a word of warning though: get ready for some trial and error. You're bound to get some weird results that you didn't expect – some good and some bad, but that's half the fun.

C O L D   S M O K I N G

Cold-smoking something is not going to cook it because the temperature will be under 37 °C. This is the first rule you should know, to avoid any unpleasant surprises on your dinner table. So because all you're doing is imparting a smoky flavour to the food, you need to cook it after you're done, unless you're cold-smoking cheese, butter or bacon. When you cold-smoke, the heat source is indirect. In other words, the smoke is coming from a heat source away from the food. So essentially, you need a smoke box and a smoke source.

To find out how to build a cold smoker, go to www.ultimatebraaimaster.com. (Check how we're self-promoting!) Or just google it. We'd need about ten pages to explain this to you.

HOT SMOKING

Okay, so this type of smoking is actually going to cook and smoke your food at the same time. That's because you hot-smoke over a direct heat source. The process could take anything from a couple of minutes (see how to smoke feta on page 13) to a couple of hours, depending on what you're trying to smoke. Below are two really simple ways to hot-smoke at home.

★ KETTLE BRAAI ★

The easiest way to smoke something in your backyard is by doing it in your kettle braai. Simply make a fire, then once you have hot coals, put the lid on and close the air intakes. When the fire has cooled down, scrape the coals to the side, scatter a handful of oak chips or other suitable woodchips onto the coals and place whatever you're going to smoke on the centre of the grid. The woodchips will ignite quickly because of the heat of the coals. Pop the lid back onto the braai (with the air vents slightly open). If you want a longer smoking time, I suggest you soak the chips in water for about an hour before putting them on the coals. You can also soak the chips in beer for a different flavour.

The aromas of woodchips vary, depending on the type of tree the wood comes from. For heavy smoke, use hickory chips (great for pork and beef). Medium smoke is the most popular way to go for poultry, game and fish, so use oak. For a sweeter-tasting smoke, use apple chips.

★ KASSIE ★

The kassie is great to use for roasting and baking, but because it has a lid, it's a great little smoker too. Build your own and then place the kassie on its belly straight onto medium to hot coals. Scatter oak chips on the bottom, pop in the wire rack, put whatever you want to smoke on the rack, then close the lid. This is a great way to smoke fish, cheese, butter and chicken.

Build a Kassie:
1 x 25 litre brand new and empty paint drum with lid (make sure it isn't plastic coated, for obvious reasons)
1 x wire rack that will fit sideways into the paint drum
wood chips for smoking
a braai fire
It's really that simple!

HOT-SMOKED BARBEL

BY JACQUES & NADIA

FOR THE BARBEL YOU'LL NEED:
3 barbel fillets
loads of coarse sea salt
black pepper, to taste

Dry-cure the barbel with coarse sea salt. Do this by laying the fish onto a clean surface and covering the entire fish with loads of sea salt. Press the salt firmly onto the fish so it absorbs into the skin. Leave the barbel to dry (about three to four hours, depending on the size of the fillets) then rinse the fish thoroughly under the tap. Pat the fish dry with paper towel and hang the fillets under the shade of a tree in a windy spot until tacky. Season with salt and black pepper then hot-smoke (page 124) in a kassie for 12 minutes. Take the fillets out and let them rest for a while (as long as it takes you to make the crème fraîche dressing) then hot-smoke for another ten minutes.

FOR THE DRESSING, YOU'LL NEED:
1 cup of crème fraîche
¼ cup of chives, finely chopped
juice of half a lemon
salt and black pepper, to taste

Mix all the dressing ingredients together thoroughly. Season with salt and pepper to taste.

Drizzle the fish with the crème fraîche dressing. Enjoy!

HOGSBACK

EASTERN CAPE

WHEN YOU FIRST DRIVE INTO HOGSBACK IT MIGHT FEEL LIKE YOU'VE JUST ENTERED A HIPPIE VILLAGE. WHILE THIS IS PARTIALLY TRUE (ESPECIALLY WITH A LABYRINTH AND REFERENCES TO FAIRIES AND HOBBITS IN EVERY DIRECTION YOU LOOK), IT'S ALSO A LITTLE BIT OF HEAVEN– ONLY ACCESSIBLE TO THOSE WHO DARE TAKE THE RISK OF BEING CALLED A HIPPIE FOR GOING THERE IN THE FIRST PLACE.

WHILE YOU'RE THERE, YOU'LL DEFINITELY GET TO MEET SOME INTERESTING CHARACTERS. I DARE GO AS FAR AS TO SAY THAT MANY OF THE FOLK IN HOGSBACK REALLY DO BELIEVE IN FAIRIES, AND EVEN UNICORNS, AND THAT'S FINE BY ME. IT ADDS TO THE LITTLE BIT OF CRAZY MAGIC YOU'LL EXPERIENCE.

BECAUSE THE TOWN'S SITUATED HIGH UP ON THE AMATHOLE MOUNTAINS OF THE EASTERN CAPE, WHEN YOU DRIVE UP THE PASS THE LANDSCAPE TRANSFORMS FROM ARID SCRUBLANDS DOTTED WITH XHOSA VILLAGES INTO WHAT FEELS LIKE AN ENGLISH SETTLER VILLAGE IN THE WOODS. YOU MIGHT AS WELL HAVE ARRIVED IN A DIFFERENT COUNTRY.

THOSE WHO COME HERE COME FOR THE 27 WATERFALLS, FOR THE MOUNTAIN VIEWS, FOR THE WALKS AND HIKES, FOR THE CLEAN BRISK AIR, FOR THE INDIGENOUS AFROMONTANE FORESTS, TO SEE THE CAPE PARROT, TO MINGLE WITH THE ECLECTIC ARTISTIC COMMUNITY OR SIMPLY FOR THE GREAT, AFFORDABLE AND FRIENDLY HOSPITALITY FOUND HERE.

WE WENT THERE FOR ALL OF THE ABOVE ...
AND TO BRAAI ... COWBOY STYLE.

A COUPLE OF YEARS AGO I BRAAIED A STEAK ON A SPADE AND IT TURNED OUT GREAT. THEN I THOUGHT, WHAT ELSE CAN I BRAAI ON A SPADE? AND LET ME TELL YOU, THE POSSIBILITIES ARE ENDLESS. POSSIBLY EVEN SIMPLER THAN A STEAK ON A SPADE IS A MIXED GRILL BREAKFAST, AND ONCE YOU GET THIS RIGHT, THE SPADE BECOMES YOUR OYSTER – YOU CAN MAKE FLAPJACKS, FRITTERS, FILLETS, BURGERS, NAAN BREAD … TRUTH IS, THE SPADE IS REALLY JUST AN (UN)GLORIFIED PAN, ALBEIT NOT A TEFLON-COATED ONE, AND ONE WITH A REALLY LONG HANDLE. OBVIOUSLY, GARDEN TOOLS HAVE NEVER BEEN TRADITIONAL BRAAI UTENSILS, SO YOU MIGHT ASK, WHY COOK SOMETHING ON A SPADE IN THE FIRST PLACE? THE ANSWER? WHY THE HELL NOT! IT LOOKS IMPRESSIVE AND IT'S FUN. WHICH MAKES ME WONDER … WHAT CAN I DO ON A PITCHFORK?

SPADE BREAKFAST FOR BEGINNERS

 JUSTIN BONELLO

When you cook different components, timing is the most important thing to consider. It's simple: just look at your ingredients and figure out what will take the longest to cook and what will take the shortest, then cook everything on the spade in that order.

FOR ONE MAN-SIZED MIXED GRILL, YOU'LL NEED:

a spade

a can of cooking spray

sunflower oil

a couple of rashers of free-range bacon

1 tomato, cut into thick slices

home-made baked beans (page 135)

half an onion, cut into rings

2 free-range or organic eggs

a couple of sprigs of thyme

salt and pepper, to taste

First up, find a spade (preferably a clean one and not the one you just used to dig a hole … or worse. Next, make a fire and balance the spade over it. The fire can be made on the ground (if it's safe) or in a normal braai area. Don't do it on a kettle braai … that's just weird.

Now, once the spade is nice and hot, pick it up, take it a couple of steps away from the fire and spray it with cooking spray (if you do it over the fire, chances are that you'll lose your eyebrows and most of your hair). Put the spade back onto the fire and add a splash of oil, swerving the spade around to distribute it evenly. Start by putting the bacon on – it should start sizzling immediately. Next put the thick-cut tomatoes on the spade, then the baked beans and the onion rings. Lastly, find an open spot and crack your eggs open. Keep turning everything (except the eggs) to keep it from burning. Season with thyme, salt and pepper. Once the bacon is nice and crispy, and the eggs are cooked to your liking, remove the spade from the heat and tuck in. The whole process shouldn't take longer than five minutes … and if it does, you're doing something wrong.

Next time you go camping, leave your pans behind and pack in a couple of spades instead. And no, don't tell your wife!

LOOK, LET'S FACE IT. THERE IS ABSOLUTELY NOTHING SEXY ABOUT BEANS, NO MATTER HOW MUCH CHOPPED CORIANDER YOU SPRINKLE OVER THEM. BUT THEY DO TASTE GOOD. THEY'RE CHEAP TO MAKE. AND THEY MAKE PERFECT SENSE FOR CAMPING TRIPS. THIS IS GUY FOOD AND SHOULD DEFINITELY ONLY BE EATEN IN THE GREAT OUTDOORS ... AND YOU REALLY SHOULDN'T SHARE A COSY LITTLE TENT WITH ANYONE. AND THAT'S ALL I'LL SAY ABOUT BEANS.

C O W B O Y   B E A N S

 JUSTIN BONELLO

Heat a glug of oil in a saucepan and fry the onion, the chopped and whole thyme sprigs and the cumin until soft and fragrant. Stir through tomato paste and cook for a minute.

Add all the tomatoes, garlic, chopped and whole chillies, sugar and vinegar. Season to taste and simmer gently for eight to ten minutes or until slightly thickened. Stir through all the drained beans, adjust the seasoning and heat through.

SERVE IT

★ Serve the beans on toast, sprinkled with some chopped coriander, basil or parsley.

★ Make little hollows in between the beans while they're still simmering, crack in a couple of eggs, pop the lid on, reduce the heat and let the eggs poach gently.

★ Scoop the beans back into the empty bean cans, eat with spoons and talk about how hard life is while sitting around a crackling fire (chewing and spitting out tobacco is optional).

YOU'LL NEED:

a glug of vegetable oil

1 onion, chopped

2 tablespoons of thyme, chopped – plus a couple of extra sprigs, kept whole

2 teaspoons of ground cumin

2 tablespoons of tomato paste

about 3 handfuls of cherry tomatoes

1 can of whole or chopped tomatoes

2–3 garlic cloves, crushed

2 fresh chillies – 1 finely chopped and 1 whole

2 teaspoons of sugar

2–3 tablespoons of red wine vinegar

salt and black pepper, to taste

1 can of butterbeans, drained

1 can of kidney beans, drained

1 can of cannellini beans, drained

ONE OF THE EASIEST DISHES YOU CAN DO ON THE FIRE IS A POTATO, WRAPPED IN FOIL, STRAIGHT IN THE COALS. BUT WHY BE SO BORING? BOTH THE POTATO AND THE SWEET POTATO ARE VEGETABLES THAT ARE BEGGING TO BE PLAYED WITH. IF YOU CAN DO A STUFFED BAKED POTATO IN THE OVEN, WHY CAN'T YOU DO IT ON THE FIRE? WELL, YOU CAN AND THAT'S THE POINT OF THIS RECIPE.

HASSLEBACK SPUDS

 JUSTIN BONELLO

The flavour possibilities are endless and if you get creative, your vegetarian friends might love you enough to wash the dishes when you're done. These are three of my favourite combinations, but go ahead and create your own.

STEP 1: Count your friends and allocate one potato or sweet potato to each.

STEP 2: Wash the spuds.

STEP 3: Cut slices into the spuds, widthways, stopping about 1 cm from the bottom.

STEP 4: Decide what you are going to stuff in between the slices.

STEP 5: Once stuffed, wrap the spuds into foil (shiny side in).

STEP 6: Pop the spuds into the coals (probably the ones you're busy braaiing your meat on) and turn them frequently to make sure they don't burn. They should cook for about 45 minutes, but once they're soft, it's time to take them off the heat. Also, bear in mind that sweet potatoes cook faster than potatoes, so if you're doing a combination of both, put the sweet potatoes into the fire about 15 minutes later.

★ SWEET POTATO WITH CAMEMBERT & ROSEMARY

Slice the cheese and roughly chop up some fresh rosemary. Put a slice of Camembert and some rosemary in between each sweet potato slice. Drizzle olive oil over the potato to prevent the cheese from sticking to the foil.

★ POTATO WITH BUTTER & SAGE

Roughly chop up a small handful of sage and using a fork, mush it with a couple of knobs of butter. Once the butter is creamy and soft, scoop lashings of it in between the potato slices. Really good with sweet potato too.

★ POTATO WITH BACON, ONION, CHEDDAR & CHILLI

Fry off a couple of streaks of chopped bacon, a medium onion (sliced) and two chopped chillies. Mix it all together and stuff it into sliced potato. Top with grated cheddar cheese, a drizzle of olive oil and more chillies if you like it hot.

THE EASTERN CAPE HIGHLANDS OF SOUTH AFRICA ARE CENTRED AROUND THE PICTURESQUE TOWN OF RHODES, ONE OF THE BEST-KEPT SECRETS OF A TRULY BEAUTIFUL COUNTRYSIDE. FOR THOSE IN THE KNOW, THERE ARE OVER 350 KM OF PRISTINE CRYSTAL CLEAR RIVERS AND STREAMS TO FLY-FISH FOR BOTH RAINBOW AND BROWN TROUT. UP IN THE HIGHLANDS ITSELF, HUNTERS RETURN YEAR IN AND YEAR OUT FOR THE BEST GREY-WINGED FRANCOLIN SHOOTING IN SOUTHERN AFRICA. WHEN YOU VISIT RHODES VILLAGE, GO AND SWITCH OFF FROM THE GRIND OF DAILY URBAN LIFE. IT IS A BEAUTIFULLY RAW AND UNTOUCHED LAND.

BUT MAKE NO MISTAKE – AS BEAUTIFUL AS THIS COUNTRYSIDE CAN BE, LOCALS WILL TELL YOU THAT THERE ARE SUDDEN THUNDERSTORMS IN SUMMER AND, IN WINTER, FIERCE BLIZZARDS WHERE THE TEMPERATURE CAN AND DOES DROP BELOW ZERO IN A HEARTBEAT.

WE HAD TWO REASONS FOR COMING TO RHODES. ONE, TO GET OUR FIRST TASTE OF THE GREY-WINGED FRANCOLIN. AND THE SECOND? TO GO SKIING ON THE SLOPES OF THE TIFFINDELL SKI RESORT.

★

1

IF RHODES WAS A COUNTRY AND COULD HAVE A NATIONAL BIRD, THE GREY-WINGED FRANCOLIN WOULD BE IT. PRETTY TO LOOK AT. PRETTY GOOD TO EAT. YOU SEE, THE NORTH-EASTERN CAPE IS FAMOUS FOR ITS WING SHOOTING OF THE GREY-WINGED FRANCOLIN. YEAR IN AND YEAR OUT, HUNTERS AND THEIR LOYAL, BIRD-SNIFFING ENGLISH POINTERS RETURN TO THE RHODES AREA FOR THIS POPULAR SPORT. SEEING THAT WE WERE IN THE AREA, IT SEEMED FITTING TO PUT SOME OF THESE BIRDS ON OUR PLATES.

GREY-WINGED FRANCOLIN BRAAI PIE

 CHRIS & SIMON

★ BRAISE THE BIRDS

Brown the birds on hot coals, turning often so they don't burn. Add a little bit of olive oil to a number 3 potjie then fry the onion, bacon, garlic, celery and carrots until the onion is soft and the bacon cooked. Add to this the chicken stock, the glass of wine, the herbs and the birds. Simmer gently until the meat is tender. Carefully take the now tender birds out of the braising liquid, wait for them to cool down to touching temperature, then pull the meat off the bones and set aside.

YOU'LL NEED:

3 Grey-winged Francolins, plucked and cleaned (if you'd like to make this at home and there are no Grey-winged Francolins flying around your garden, use 1 free-range chicken instead)

a glug of olive oil

1 red onion, chopped coarsely

a handful of bacon, chopped

2 garlic cloves, crushed and chopped

2 celery stalks, chopped

a handful of carrots, chopped

750 ml chicken stock

1 glass of red wine (drink the rest, but keep the empty bottle)

a handful of fresh thyme and rosemary

★ THE FILLING

Slowly caramelise the onion in a glug of olive oil and a couple of pinches of sugar, then add the garlic, mushrooms, thyme, salt and pepper. Keep stirring until the mushrooms have browned. In a separate pot, reduce the braising liquid to about half, then add the cream and all the other ingredients, including the meat. The filling must be moist, NOT wet, otherwise the pastry will become soggy. While the filling is cooling down, make the pastry.

YOU'LL NEED:

1 white onion, finely chopped

a glug of olive oil

a couple of pinches of sugar

1 or 2 garlic cloves, crushed and chopped

about 1 cup of large black mushrooms, sliced

2 teaspoons of thyme, finely chopped

salt and cracked black pepper, to taste

½ cup of cream

about 2-3 cups of the braising liquid, strained

a couple of fried bacon bits from the braising liquid

★ ROUGH PUFF

Sieve the flour and salt into a mixing bowl. Add the butter and water and combine. Form a ball of dough with your hands, wrap in cling wrap and put it in the fridge to chill for about 30 minutes. After half an hour put the dough on a floured surface, grab that (now-empty) red wine bottle and roll the dough into a rectangle. Brush with some of the melted butter, fold the sides closed towards to the middle, and then roll it out again. Repeat this buttering, folding and rolling process as many times as you can until you are gatvol. Keep putting it back into the fridge in between, otherwise the pastry will just become an oily mess. Allow the pastry (and yourself) to chill for about 25 minutes.

YOU'LL NEED:

500 g cake flour

a pinch of salt

250 g butter, grated

300 ml water, iced

½ cup of melted butter

★ THE PIE

Finally! You're almost done, rock star! Cut the pastry into halves, scoop equal amounts of the filling onto each half, then fold the pastry over the filling in the shape of half moons (like a Cornish pasty), and close it by pressing the edges with a fork. Make sure the pies are completely sealed, otherwise the filling will spill out, and after all that hard work you might fall apart too. Prick some holes into the top of the pies with a fork to allow the steam to escape while the pie is cooking.

★ THE BRAAI

Carefully place the pies in a sandwich grid. A good idea is to brush the grid with oil to prevent the pastry from sticking, but Simon and Chris say you shouldn't close the grid AT ALL. Up to you. Braai over medium to low coals until the pastry is cooked and a lovely golden brown.

Tuck in.

2

TIFFINDELL

You know how some horror movies are just so predictable?
That's how my crew and I felt when we were travelling up to
Tiffindell in the back of a makeshift bakkie / people-carrier.

Let me paint the scene for you:

Six relatively young and relatively good-looking film crew
members (it's a B-grade horror) get into the back of an
unmarked white bakkie, of course never meeting the driver.
Once they are all seated and as the bakkie pulls off, the
writer of the group starts looking around inside. (She's got
great female intuition and is the smarter one of the group.)
To her horror, she realises that the back door can't open
from the inside. And that there are prison-type bars covering
the windows. There's no way out. The car is driving fast
(reaaaaally fast) as it expertly navigates the switchbacks
deeper and deeper into the snow-covered valley, winding up
impossibly steep roads. It's not a comfortable ride, with
a lot of clanging and banging going on. The film crew can
barely sit and have to clutch on to each other, the prison
bars and their seats, trying their best not to fall over.
They try to see out the windows, but the combination of their
scared heavy breathing and the cold outside has frosted up
the windows, making it impossible to see anything. After 30
minutes of blind driving (which feels like a lifetime to the
food stylist who has been sitting, shivering in the corner),
the car comes to an abrupt stop. They hear the crunch of the
driver's footsteps as he walks beside the car to open up the
back. The door opens and to everyone's surprise, they have
travelled to …

… a ski lodge in the middle of South Africa!

The rest of our 'horror movie' has a very sweet ending, with
chocolate mug cakes and an array of hot desserts in the most
spectacular snowy landscape. And yes … it was all done on the
braai.

End scene.

IF YOU ASK ME WHICH TWO THINGS ARE QUINTESSENTIALLY CAPE TOWN, I'LL TELL YOU IT'S WATCHING THE STORMERS PLAY AND LONG STREET ... BUT MOSTLY, JUST THE STORMERS ... ESPECIALLY WHEN WE WIN. FOR BERTUS, THE TWO THINGS THAT DEFINE THE MOTHER CITY FOR HIM ARE ROTIS AND BOEBER. THIS CAPE MALAY HOT DRINK IS FRAGRANT AND THE PERFECT PUDDING TO SLURP ON AROUND A BONFIRE ON A COLD WINTER'S NIGHT.

BOEBER

 BERTUS BASSON

NOT THAT BOEBER – THIS IS THE DRINKING KIND...

YOU'LL NEED:

a flat-bottomed potjie pot

1 litre of milk

a couple of cinnamon sticks

1 vanilla pod, scraped with the stalk

160 g sugar

a big handful of raisins

a small handful of cardamom pods

zest of half a lemon

a handful of vermicelli or rice

Heat up the milk until boiling then reduce it to let the milk simmer slowly. Add the cinnamon, vanilla seeds and pod, sugar, raisins, cardamom and lemon zest. Stir and let it cook for about ten minutes until all the spices have released their flavour and the milk is beautifully aromatic. Add a handful of vermicelli and stir again. (Instead of vermicelli you can also use rice – the idea is that the starch will thicken the milk.) Once the milk is a lovely custardy consistency, remove it from the heat and pour it into cups. Before sipping, warn your friends to do it through their teeth, otherwise they might end up crunching down on a whole cinnamon stick or cardamom pod ... or don't warn them – depending on your mood and their behaviour.

RHODES

146

THIS IS ONE OF THE MOST DELICIOUS TARTS
YOU WILL EVER GET YOUR HANDS ON! (NO
... NOT LIKE THAT – GET YOUR BRAIN OUT OF
THE GUTTER!) IT'S THAT PERFECT SCENARIO
WHERE SWEET AND CRUNCHY MEETS SOUR
AND CREAMY. TOPPED WITH FRESH FRUIT
AND DUSTED WITH ICING SUGAR, THIS LEMON
TART IS THE BERRIES!

FIRE-BAKED LEMON TART

 TOMAS & DANIEL

⭐ SWEET PASTRY BASE

YOU'LL NEED:
250 g unsalted butter
140 g castor sugar
2 eggs – plus the yolk of 1 egg
500 g flour

Start by creaming the butter and sugar in a mixing
bowl. Carefully mix in the two whole eggs and stir
in the flour. Once you have a ball of dough, let it
rest in the fridge for about two hours.

Roll out the dough and line a tart base, then bake
over moderate coals in a kettle braai (lid on) until
golden brown (this should take about ten minutes).
If you have a kassie (page 124), then you can also
use that. Take the tart base off the heat, brush with
egg yolk and return to the heat for another two to
three minutes until set.

⭐ LEMON FILLING

YOU'LL NEED:
6 eggs
200 g castor sugar
juice of 4 lemons
400 ml double cream
a small handful or raspberries and blueberries
a sprinkling of icing sugar

Whisk together the eggs and sugar, then add the
lemon juice and mix well. Stir in the cream, then
pour the filling into the sweet pastry base and
bake over cool coals in a kettle braai or kassie for
about ten to 15 minutes until it's just set. Take the
tart off the heat and set aside – you'll notice that
the filling is still slightly soft, but it will continue to
cook for a couple of minutes after you've removed
it. Allow to cool completely, then top the tart with
fresh raspberries and blueberries and dust with
icing sugar.

Thanks, guys – it's not often I say this, but this tart
is a keeper!

TO EVERYONE'S DELIGHT, ETIENNE AND HEIN MADE THIS PUDDING A COUPLE OF TIMES WHILE WE WERE ON THE ROAD. IF YOU'RE IN THE GREAT OUTDOORS, IN THE MIDDLE OF WINTER, THERE'S SOMETHING INCREDIBLY SOOTHING ABOUT EATING WARM CHOCOLATE CAKE STRAIGHT OUT OF A MUG. THANKS, GUYS!

WET CHOCOLATE CAKE MUGS

 ETIENNE & HEIN

★ THE DARK CHOCOLATE GANACHE

Heat the cream in a saucepan over moderate coals. Add the blocks of chocolate, and keep stirring until the chocolate has melted. Take it off the heat and whisk. Put the ganache in a ziplock bag and put it in the snow (or fridge) to cool.

YOU'LL NEED:

500 ml fresh cream

1 slab of dark chocolate, broken into blocks

ziplock bag

★ THE CAKE MUGS

Cream the eggs and one cup of castor sugar in a mixing bowl. Mix the boiling water and cocoa powder together before combining with the eggs. Sieve together the salt, baking powder and flour, then combine it with the cocoa-egg mixture until there are no lumps and it's completely smooth. Stir in the oil and almond shavings. Take some butter and thoroughly grease about six enamel cups. Pour the chocolate batter into the cups (just a little over the halfway mark) then pop the cups onto the grid of a kettle braai (with the lid on) over moderate coals (ideally the temperature should be at about 180 °C) for 20 to 25 minutes.

While the mug cakes are baking, mix about half a cup of cherry syrup, a quarter cup of castor sugar and the brandy in a saucepan and simmer for about five minutes, or until the sugar has completely dissolved. Once the mug cakes are baked, pour the brandy mixture over the cakes, then scoop about two tablespoons (or more) of dark chocolate ganache on each mug cake. Finish with a cherry or two on top. Serve immediately! If you're a guy, you just got massive braai kudos, and if you're a lady, you've just become the Nigella Lawson of the braai. These cakes are spectacular!

YOU'LL NEED:

3 eggs

1¼ cup of castor sugar

125 ml water, boiling

60 ml cocoa powder

5 ml salt

15 ml baking powder

1 cup of cake flour

40 ml oil

½ cup of almond shavings

a few knobs of butter

6 enamel mugs

maraschino cherries with syrup

½ cup of Klipdrift Premium brandy

AMARULA AND CHOCOLATE PANCAKE CAKE

 JUSTIN BONELLO

★ THE BATTER

YOU'LL NEED:

4 cups of flour

½ cup of sugar

a drizzle of sunflower oil

4–5 free-range or organic eggs

about 1 litre of milk

First up, make a batch of pancake batter. Put the flour, sugar and sunflower oil into a mixing bowl, make a well in the middle then crack the eggs into the well. Next, using a wooden spoon, mix it together until you've got a sticky dough. Now start adding the milk a splash at a time. Every time you add milk, mix it into the batter, then once fully absorbed, add more milk again. Keep doing this until you've used all the milk and have batter just a little thinner than syrup. Put a butter-greased pan onto a medium heat and pour in about half a ladle of batter, spreading it evenly all over the pan. When it's cooked through, flip it over and brown the other side. Repeat until you've used up all the batter, but keep greasing and wiping the pan between pancakes.

★ AMARULA MASCARPONE

YOU'LL NEED:

4 cups of mascarpone

1 cup of Amarula

½ cup of icing sugar

Mix all the ingredients together in one bowl.

★ BALSAMIC AND MINT STRAWBERRIES

YOU'LL NEED:

1 kg strawberries, quartered

1 cup of castor sugar

150 ml balsamic vinegar

2 handfuls of chopped mint

In a third bowl, mix these ingredients together and leave to stand for an hour.

★ CHOCOLATE GANACHE

YOU'LL NEED:

500 g chocolate, melted

350 ml cream, warmed

2 teaspoons of vanilla essence

In another bowl, whisk these ingredients together.

★ BUTTERSCOTCH SAUCE

YOU'LL NEED:

2 cups of sugar

1½ cups of cream

200 g butter

2 teaspoons of vanilla essence

In a pan, heat and melt the sugar until it's a lovely caramel colour, then add and keep stirring in the other ingredients until everything's melted and combined.

★ STACK IT

You should have quite an impressive stack of pancakes to play with now and there really are no rules for how to build the best pancake cake. This is how I do it, but you can mix it up.

Lay a pancake flat and spread generously with chocolate ganache. Spread Amarula mascarpone onto four pancakes, roll them up and arrange on top of the ganache pancake. Drizzle the rolled up pancakes with butterscotch sauce. Cover with another flat pancake, ganache and four more rolled-up mascarpone pancakes. Keep repeating this until you have only one pancake left to layer over the top. Spread the remaining mascarpone onto this, cover with the strawberries, a little grated chocolate and you're ready to tuck in. How you manage to eat this awesome monstrosity is up to you. It's a bit childish really, but oh-so good.

SHOWING PART OF SOUTHERN AFRICA WITH
SOME ROADS AND PLACES AND WITH
BOUNDARIES NATURAL REPLACING NATIONAL

1:2,000,000

| 0 km | | 100 km | | 200 km |
| distance | | 5 cm | | 10 cm |

| 0 m | 1000 m | 2000 m | 3000 m |
| elevation | | | |

IF YOU'VE NEVER BEEN TO THE TRANSKEI COAST, I'M ALMOST HESITANT TO GIVE YOU DIRECTIONS. THIS PIECE OF HEAVEN, WHICH STRETCHES FROM THE KEI RIVER IN THE SOUTH TO PORT EDWARD IN THE NORTH, IS WHERE I HAVE SOME OF MY FONDEST MEMORIES GROWING UP. EACH YEAR I FIND MYSELF RETURNING HERE, AND AN 8000-KM CROSS-COUNTRY ROAD TRIP WAS ANOTHER PERFECT EXCUSE TO HEAD BACK, LET MY HAIR DOWN, KICK OFF MY SHOES, GRAB MY FISHING ROD AND WANDER.

Generally, I think it's safe to say that South Africa has some of the most beautiful beaches in the world and most South Africans pack up for December holidays and go on an annual trek up or down the coast (depending which way you hold the map) to their favourite seaside destinations. And come to think of it, so do I. But the big difference is my seaside spot isn't overcrowded, doesn't smell like coconut oil and when I walk on the beach, there's the very real danger that I actually might cut my foot on a seashell ... because in the Transkei there are millions of them scattered everywhere.

For many people the idea of coming across a lone cow on the beach might be a little weird, but let me tell you, that suits me just fine. And if you don't like walking for hours with nothing more than your own thoughts for company, then this is definitely not the place for you. And the drive there? Horrific! There are so many potholes – some bigger than your car – that it's definitely not the type of road you should dare drive on in your souped-up BMW with low profiles. In fact, rather just stay away. This is my piece of paradise, and I'd like to keep it that way. But if you're a spirited adventurer, the Transkei is right up your alley.

On arrival – and after what seemed like a lifetime in Iceland (Rhodes Village) – the first thing I did before even climbing out of my car, was kick off my snow boots and three pairs of thermal socks, roll up my jeans (and long johns) and throw my jacket, scarf and beanie behind the seat. I speed-walked down to the beach (faster than a Sandton housewife) and submerged my toes in the warm golden sand at Seagulls Beach Resort. Once my feet and brain had defrosted, it was the perfect afternoon for a couple of rounds of poker, braaied tapas and good old brandy and Coke – my not-at-all-fancy-but-will-do-just-fine sundowner cocktail solution. And the rest? Well, it's a bit of a sea breeze really.

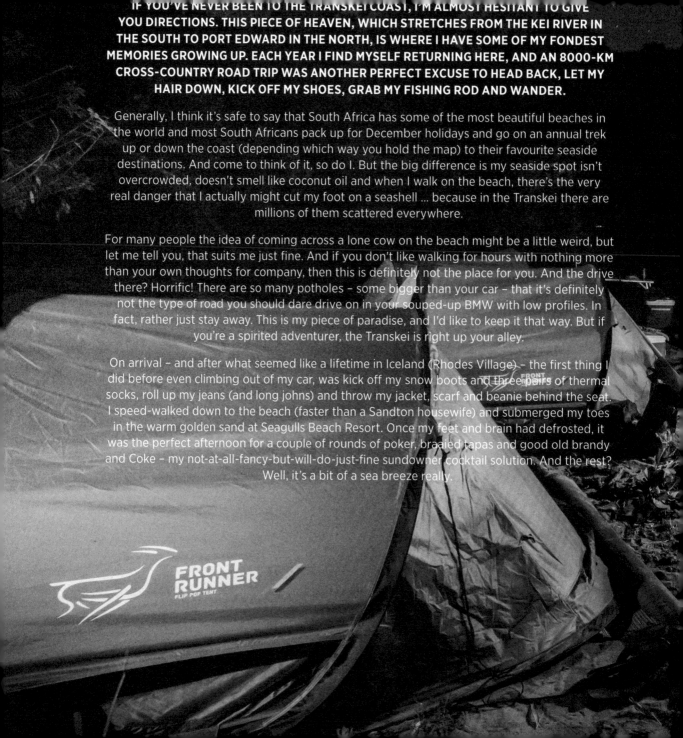

FRONT RUNNER
FLIP POP TENT

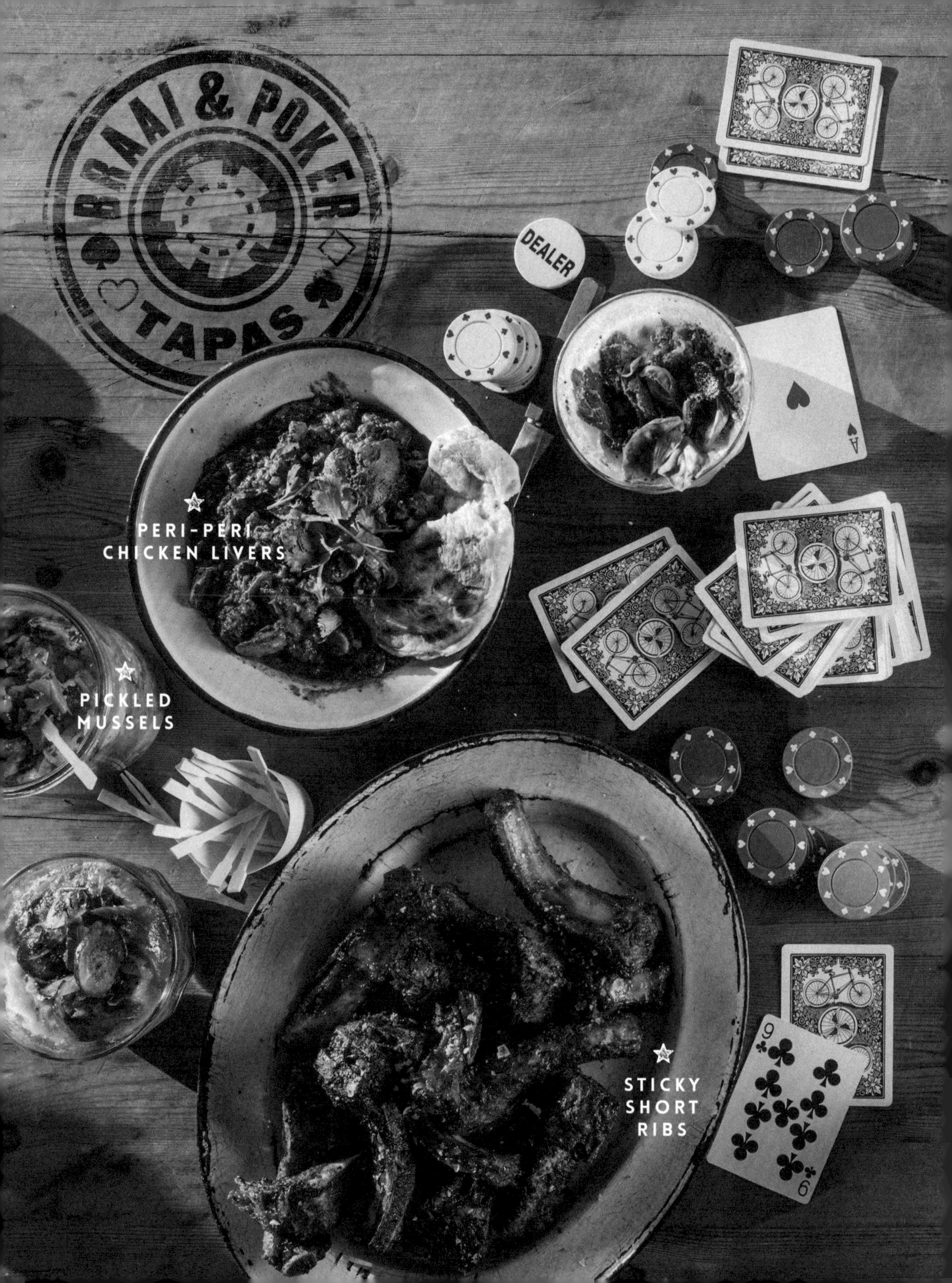
BRAAI & POKER
TAPAS
DEALER
PERI-PERI
CHICKEN LIVERS
PICKLED
MUSSELS
STICKY
SHORT
RIBS

FIRE-BAKED
CAMEMBERT
POTS

NAAN
BREAD

THIS RECIPE WILL MAKE ABOUT SIX NAAN BREADS, SO DOUBLE OR TRIPLE UP, DEPENDING ON HOW MANY HUNGRY FRIENDS ARE SITTING AROUND YOUR TABLE.

NAAN BREAD

 JUSTIN BONELLO

YOU'LL NEED:

150 ml milk

10 ml castor sugar

5 g dried yeast

450 g bread flour

5 ml salt

5 ml baking powder

30 ml vegetable oil, plus a little extra

150 ml yogurt

1 egg, lightly beaten

2 garlic cloves, very finely chopped

10 ml toasted cumin seeds, bashed

5 ml coriander seeds, bashed

MAKE THE DOUGH...

Start by heating the milk until warm, then add half the castor sugar and all the yeast. Stir and set aside in a warm place for about ten to 15 minutes or until frothy. Next, sift the flour, salt, baking powder and remaining castor sugar into a large bowl. Stir through the frothy yeast mixture, vegetable oil, yogurt, egg, garlic, cumin and coriander. Mix this until you have a ball of dough. Put the dough onto a clean surface and knead for about ten minutes or until smooth and elastic. Grease the dough with a drop of oil, place it in a bowl, cover and set aside until it's doubled in size (about an hour). Punch down the dough, knead it again and then divide the dough into six equal balls (or 12 or 18 if you've doubled or tripled the recipe).

Take one ball at a time, and shape it into what you imagine a tear would look like if it were bread. Make these tears roughly the size of your hand (unless you have teeny-tiny hands) and about 5 mm thick. While you're working with one ball of dough, keep the rest covered to prevent them from drying out. You should be able to fry about two naan breads at a time. Preheat the biggest fireproof pan you've got over moderate coals. Add a splash of oil, swirl it around to cover the entire surface of the pan, then quickly wipe off the excess oil to grease the pan. Pop your first naan bread into the pan and fry until the bottom is golden and crispy. Don't press down on the bread with a spatula – it will lose all it's delicious fluffiness. Once the underside of the bread is done, flip it over to fry the other side. The whole frying process should take about three to five minutes. Once the first batch is done, take the breads out of the pan, brush one side with melted butter and keep warm. Repeat until you've used up all the dough. These breads are best when they're eaten within an hour of making them.

THIS IS A SERIOUSLY GREAT SNACK – AN EASY WAY TO STRETCH THE MUSSEL, AND A DELICIOUS DISH ON A TAPAS MENU. IF YOU HAVE EXTRA, YOU CAN KEEP THEM SEALED IN A BOTTLE IN YOUR FRIDGE FOR ABOUT A WEEK.

PICKLED MUSSELS

 JUSTIN BONELLO

Take a large potjie pot and place it over moderate coals. Add the mussels, a dash of water and the white wine, and steam them until they've opened. Discard any mussels that haven't opened. Reserve about a third of a cup of the sweet mussel juice that's at the bottom of the potjie pot. Get a friend to patiently take the meat out of the shells while you make the marinade (remind them that the beards have to be removed too).

Heat olive oil in a fireproof non-stick saucepan and gently soften the carrot, chilli, onion, rosemary, thyme, paprika and grated lemon peel for about a minute, or until fragrant. Add the garlic, tomato, lemon juice, salt and reserved mussel juice, and simmer for a couple of minutes to infuse the flavour.

Stir in the parsley, sherry vinegar, chopped chives and an extra glug of olive oil. Have a taste – if it's not acidic enough, add a couple of splashes of white balsamic vinegar.

Take it off the heat and leave to cool slightly. Pour the marinade over the mussels then scoop the mussels and the marinade into good old sterilised Consol jars. Refrigerate for at least three hours, but preferably overnight. Serve straight out the jar with crispy bread.

YOU'LL NEED:

2 kg mussels, scrubbed and beards removed

a dash of water

a couple of glugs of white wine

3 tablespoons of olive oil

1 carrot, grated

1 chilli, finely chopped

1 onion, finely chopped

½ tablespoon of finely chopped rosemary

1 tablespoon of chopped thyme

1 teaspoon of smoked paprika

juice and grated peel of 1 lemon

2–3 garlic cloves, minced

2 tomatoes, roughly chopped

a couple of pinches salt

¼ cup of parsley, chopped

⅓ cup of sherry vinegar

¼ cup of chives, finely chopped

white balsamic vinegar (optional)

J

45671

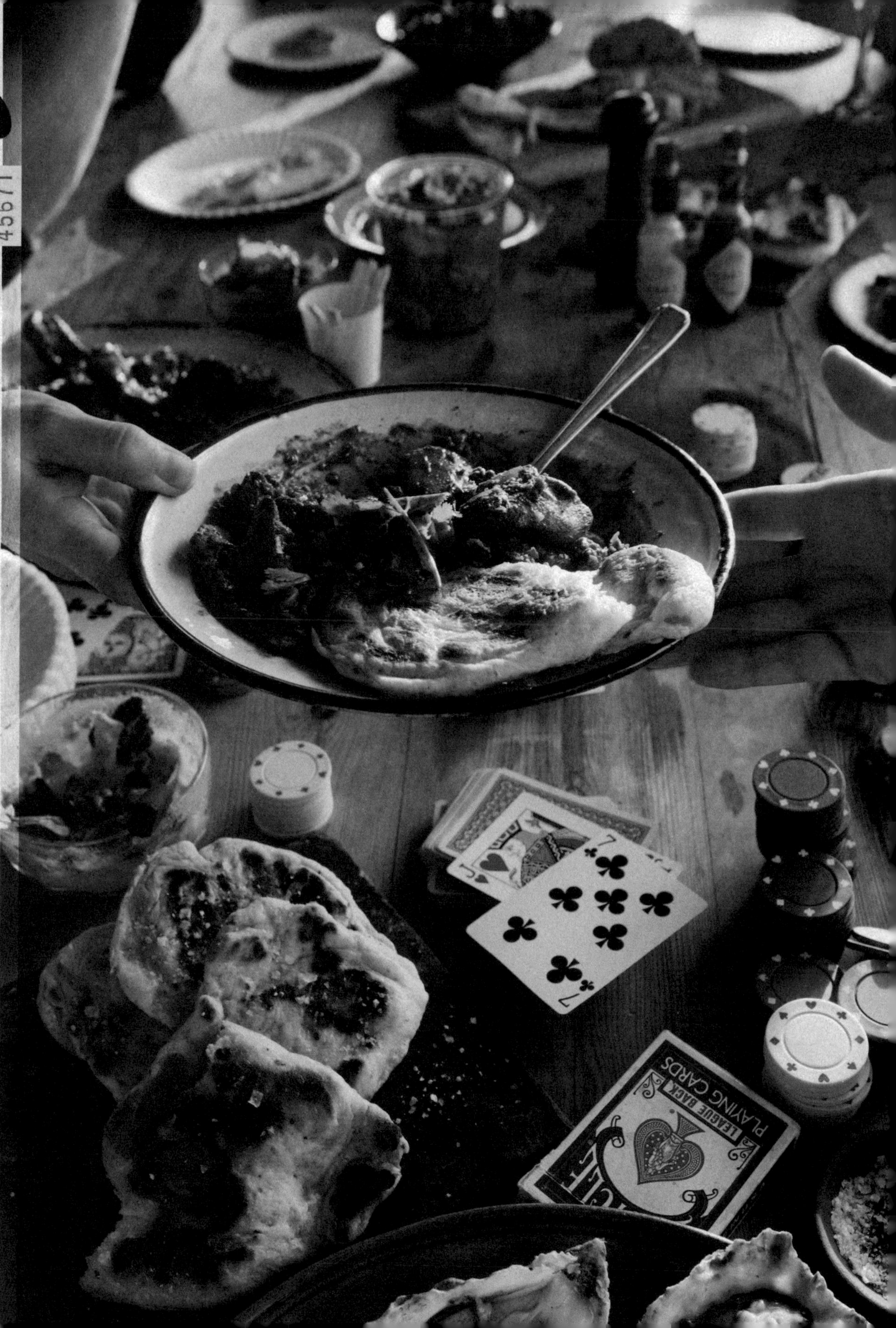

**I'VE FINALLY PERFECTED THE PERI-PERI CHICKEN LIVER RECIPE!
IT'S GOT THE RIGHT AMOUNT OF HEAT, SPICE AND SAUCE. AND THE GREAT THING?
IT DOESN'T HAVE TO COST AN ARM AND A LEG (AND A KIDNEY) TO MAKE.**

PERI-PERI CHICKEN LIVERS

 JUSTIN BONELLO

The worst thing you can do is overcook chicken livers – they end up rubbery and dry. The idea is to season the livers with salt and pepper then to flash-fry them in a pan with a splash of olive oil and butter so they're sealed on all sides but still bloody on the inside. Once you've done this, take them off the heat and set aside until later. Next, heat olive oil in a large non-stick pan over moderate coals. Add the onion, thyme, chilli, peri-peri spice, cumin and paprika, and cook gently until the onion is soft. Next, stir in the tomato paste and fry for about a minute. You'll notice the onions and spices have now started sticking to the bottom of the pan, so add the red wine vinegar to deglaze the pan. Now add the chopped tomatoes, chicken stock, bay leaves, salt and pepper and a splash of white wine. Stir and leave to simmer until you've got a sauce resembling loose chutney. (This should take about 30 minutes.) If the tomato mixture is too thick, add a couple of splashes of water to loosen it. Now it's time to add the chicken livers that have been resting on the side, along with the lemon juice and zest, brandy and sliced pickled garlic. Simmer gently for about ten minutes. By now the livers should be tender, but not raw, so take them off the heat, stir in a glug of good olive oil and serve with fresh naan bread – great for scooping and dipping!

YOU'LL NEED:

3 tubs of free-range chicken livers, cleaned

salt and cracked pepper, to taste

a couple of glugs of olive oil

a decent knob of butter

1 onion, finely chopped

about 4 tablespoons of thyme, chopped

1 chilli, finely chopped

1 tablespoon of peri-peri spice

1 teaspoon of ground cumin

2 teaspoons of paprika

1 tablespoon of tomato paste

⅓ cup of red wine vinegar

3–4 ripe tomatoes, chopped

⅓ cup of chicken stock

a couple of bay leaves

a splash of white wine

juice and grated peel of 1 lemon

a splash of brandy (optional)

8 or more pickled garlic cloves, thinly sliced

BECAUSE THE RIBS NEED TO SIMMER AND THEN MARINATE OVERNIGHT, THESE BABIES TAKE A LITTLE EFFORT, BUT I PROMISE YOU THEY'RE THE MOST FLAVOURFUL, STICKIEST AND TENDER LIP-SMACKING RIBS YOU'LL EVER GET YOUR HANDS ON! SERVE AS PART OF A TAPAS MENU, OR BY ITSELF AS A SNACK BEFORE THE BRAAI.

STICKY SHORT RIBS

 JUSTIN BONELLO

THE NIGHT BEFORE...

Grab the biggest pot you have, fill it with water to about halfway and bring to the boil. Once boiling, reduce the heat, add the garlic, soy sauce, lime juice and ginger, then the blocks of ribs. Simmer gently for about 45 minutes to an hour, then remove from the heat and allow the ribs to cool in the water (to infuse with the flavours), then strain.

While the ribs are simmering, make the marinade. Make double!

Pour the sugar and sherry into a saucepan and simmer until the sugar has melted. Next, stir in the remainder of the ingredients and let it simmer for about 15 minutes. Put the ribs in a large Tupperware, pour over half the sauce, pop the lid on, shake it around a bit so that the marinade covers all the meat and leave it in the fridge overnight. Bottle the other half of the marinade to use as extra basting sauce.

THE NEXT DAY ...

The next day, get ready to wow your friends with the best ribs they've ever eaten. Place the ribs on a grid over moderate coals and slowly braai them, turning and basting with the extra marinade you made as you go, for about 30 to 40 minutes or until caramelised and sticky. Give them one last generous brush of basting sauce without turning them over again, take them off the heat and serve.

YOU'LL NEED:

a couple of garlic cloves, bashed

a couple of splashes of Kikkoman soy sauce

1 lime, halved and squeezed

a knob of ginger, roughly chopped

2 kg pork loin rib racks, cut into blocks of 4 (ask your butcher to do this for you)

FOR THE MARINADE, YOU'LL NEED:

about ⅓ cup soft brown sugar

about ¼ cup of sherry

a couple of chunks of ginger, peeled and finely grated

1 red chilli, finely chopped

about 3 garlic cloves, crushed and chopped

1 cup of tomato sauce

a couple of splashes of Worcester sauce

a couple of tablespoons of Dijon mustard

a good couple of splashes of Kikkoman soy sauce

juice of about 4 lemons

salt and pepper, to taste

166

STUFF THESE WITH DIFFERENT GOODIES. WHEN I SAY 'STUFF', I MEAN SCORE THE TOP OF THE CHEESE WITH A SHARP KNIFE AND POKE THE INGREDIENTS INTO THE CHEESE IN ANY WAY THAT ACTUALLY WORKS FOR YOU.

FIRE-BAKED CAMEMBERT POTS

 JUSTIN BONELLO

Combine the different variations in individual ramekins and place the ramekins in a flat-bottomed potjie. Fill the potjie with water just halfway up the ramekins. Pop the lid on, scatter with a couple of coals and place the potjie over moderate coals. Bake for about 15 to 20 minutes or until the inside of the Camembert is all melted and gooey inside. Serve with crackers or fresh bread, or just stick your finger into it (unless you're sharing with friends).

Also, if you don't feel like being that fancy, you can bake the Camembert plain … it's just as good! But really, make some naan bread (page 162).

CAMEMBERT STUFFED WITH:

★ a couple of leaves of sage and sliced garlic, then scattered with pine nuts, a splash of olive oil and Maldon salt and pepper to taste.

★ sliced preserved figs, shavings of Parma ham and rosemary, lightly drizzled with olive oil and seasoned with Maldon salt and black pepper.

★ moist, sliced biltong, sprigs of fresh thyme and sliced garlic, lightly drizzled with olive oil and seasoned with Maldon salt and black pepper.

HEY, GUYS, LET'S PLAY POKER!!

1. Learn the rules of the game before playing.

2. Keep a straight face ALL THE TIME.

3. Hustle.

4. Make eye contact – keep it for as long as possible. Stare your opponent down.

5. Fake confidence by placing high bets – this is sure to make some players fold. K*k idea if you don't have a good hand.

6. Never ever let anyone know that you have a bad hand. In the world of poker, you have no friends. Ever. Not even your wife.

7. Always have good whiskey, cigars and snacks on the table.

8. Don't bet or play if you don't think you can win the round.

9. Never show your cards if you don't have to. If everyone else folds before you do, just put your cards back in the deck.

10. The first person out of the game becomes the permanent dealer. And drinks pourer.

11. Learn a couple of chip tricks – even if you don't play a lot, it gives the impression that you do. Learn to do tricks like 'the shuffle' and 'the thumb flick'.

12. If there's a guy named Erik playing, don't ever believe anything he says.

13. Be a good winner: first buy everyone a round of drinks with your winnings and then taunt them. You've earned it.

14. Wear your best underwear … just in case, well, you know.

⭐

WHEN YOU GET TO WALK THE WILD COAST FORAGING FOR FOOD, ONE INGREDIENT YOU'RE BOUND TO FIND ARE MUSSELS. CAN YOU IMAGINE PICKING MUSSELS AND THEN PREPARING THEM RIGHT THERE ON THE BEACH WHILE THE SUN IS SETTING IN THE BACKGROUND? LIFE REALLY DOESN'T GET ANY BETTER THAN THAT. IT'S SIMPLY PERFECT. GET OUT THERE AND DO IT ... BUT MAKE SURE YOU'VE GOT A PERMIT BEFORE YOU DO – AVAILABLE FROM THE POST OFFICE.

MUSSEL CURRY

 ANDREW & THANDO

YOU'LL NEED:

1.5 kg mussels, scrubbed clean, beards removed and soaked in salted water (or sea water)

a glug of olive oil

1 onion, finely chopped

2 garlic cloves, crushed

3 red chillies, seeds removed and chopped

a chunk of ginger, grated

2 teaspoons of green curry paste

2 tablespoons of curry powder

2 tablespoons of garam masala

1 tin of whole peeled tomatoes

1 tin of coconut milk

First up, steam the clean, beardless mussels until they open up. Toss the ones that didn't open back into the ocean and set the open ones aside. Now, heat a potjie over moderate to hot coals, add a glug of olive oil and fry the onion, garlic, chilli and ginger until the onions are soft, then stir in the green curry paste. Next, chuck in all the spices, mix everything around and cook for another minute or two. Add the whole peeled tomatoes and once all the liquid has evaporated, pour in the coconut milk. Once the sauce starts to simmer, add the mussels and cook for about five minutes more. Take it off the heat and serve with freshly baked bread (great to mop up the sauce) or rice, good wine, great friends and a spectacular view of the ocean.

THIS 70S CLASSIC TOTALLY DESERVES A COMEBACK! THERE ARE LOADS OF VARIATIONS OF THE PRAWN COCKTAIL AND I CAN THINK OF TWO: THE KITSCH KIND, WHICH YOU SERVE ON TOP OF LETTUCE IN GIANT WHITE SEASHELLS, AND THE RETRO VERSION, SERVED IN MARTINI GLASSES. THIS WAS THE 'IT' STARTER AT ANY PARTY AND THE CORE INGREDIENTS WERE ALWAYS THE SAME: AVO, LETTUCE, MAYO AND PRAWNS. THE PRAWN COCKTAIL DOESN'T HAVE TO BE OUTDATED – I SUGGEST YOU GIVE IT A KICK UP THE BACKSIDE AND BRING IT BACK TO THE PARTY. THIS IS HOW KATE AND JONNO DO IT.

PRAWN COCKTAIL

 KATE & JONNO

YOU'LL NEED:

about 2 kg prawns, veins, heads and shells removed

olive oil

salt and black pepper, to taste

3 cups of mayo – if you know how to make your own, do it!

2 handfuls of fresh dill, roughly chopped

¾ large cucumber, finely cubed

juice of 2 lemons

about 4 tablespoons of Worcester sauce

2 red chillies, seeds removed and finely chopped

about 1 tablespoon of Tabasco

2 large heads of iceberg lettuce, broken up

6 ripe avocados, peeled and cut into chunky cubes

a dash of cayenne pepper

Once you've done the unthinkable and cleaned, peeled and beheaded each and every prawn, pat them dry with some paper towels and dowse with oil and lots of salt and pepper. Get a pan smoking hot over moderate to hot coals and fry the prawns in small batches. Don't put more than one layer of prawns into the pan as they will stew in their juices and you won't get that smoky grilled flavour. Remove them from the heat and allow to cool.

When all the prawns are cooked, combine the mayo with the dill, cucumber, lemon juice, Worcester sauce and chillies and season to taste. Mix the prawns through this mixture and leave to stand for an hour. Any leftover prawn juices can be added to the mixture for extra flavour. Lay the lettuce out on a platter, top with avo pieces and then with the prawn mixture. Sprinkle with a dash of cayenne pepper and dig in.

THOSE OF US BORN IN THE 70S OR WHO GREW UP IN THE 80S HAVE SOME OF THE BEST MEMORIES. YOU KNOW HOW THOSE NOSTALGIC CONVERSATIONS GO, WHEN YOU SIT AROUND WITH YOUR FRIENDS AND SOMEONE MENTIONS GOOD OLD MACGYVER, SOMETHING ALONG THE LINES OF: 'MY KID WAS STUCK INSIDE THE BATHROOM, SO I "MACGYVERED" THE DOOR OPEN.' (YES, THIS ACTUALLY HAPPENED TO ME.) BEFORE YOU KNOW IT, THE CONVERSATION STARTS FLOWING WITH TRINKETS AND GEMS OF THE 70S AND 80S. HE-MAN. SHE-RA. SCOT SCOTT. RODRIGUEZ. MY LITTLE PONY. GUMMI BEARS. NEW KIDS ON THE BLOCK. HAAS DAS. GHOST POPS. SUPER MARIO BROS. CHARM BRACELETS. PAULA ABDUL. ALF. GREMLINS. DEVILLED EGGS. FONDUE. GRAPEFRUIT FOR BREAKFAST. PRAWN COCKTAILS AT PARTIES. POP ROCKS FOR THE KIDS. IRISH COFFEES FOR DAD AND HIS FRIENDS. AND DOM PEDROS – ONE OF THE MOST FORGOTTEN-ABOUT AND UNDERRATED DESSERT DRINKS YOU CAN STILL MAKE. SO WHEN BERTUS REVIVED THEM, WE WERE IN OUR ELEMENT. THERE ARE NO REAL RULES WHEN MAKING DOM PEDROS, EXCEPT TO USE DECENT VANILLA ICE CREAM AND YOUR FAVOURITE LIQUOR. THIS RECIPE WILL NEVER BE OUTDATED AND WILL ALWAYS BE THE PERFECT SWEET ENDING TO ANY MEAL.

DOM PEDROS

 BERTUS BASSON

★ THE BASIC DOM PEDRO

YOU'LL NEED:

1 cup of good vanilla ice cream

a couple of splashes of cream

your choice of liquor – 2 shots per person

a splash of milk

a piping bag and nozzle – a star-shaped nozzle, if you have one

Put the ice cream, cream and shots of liquor into a blender and blitz until smooth. If it looks too thick, add a splash of milk and blitz again. Pour into glasses and pipe more cream on top. Add some colourful straws and sip the afternoon away.

★ HAZELNUT & AMARETTO

Add a small handful crushed hazelnuts to ice cream before blending. Sprinkle some grated chocolate on top.

★ COFFEE, KAHLUA & VODKA

Add one shot of Kahlua and one shot of vodka to each Dom Pedro, plus a shot of good (cooled) espresso. Decorate with a couple of coffee beans on top.

★ CHOCOLATE, WHISKEY & HONEY

Melt some chocolate and drizzle it onto the inside of the glass before pouring in the milkshake. Add a shot of whiskey and a teaspoon of honey.

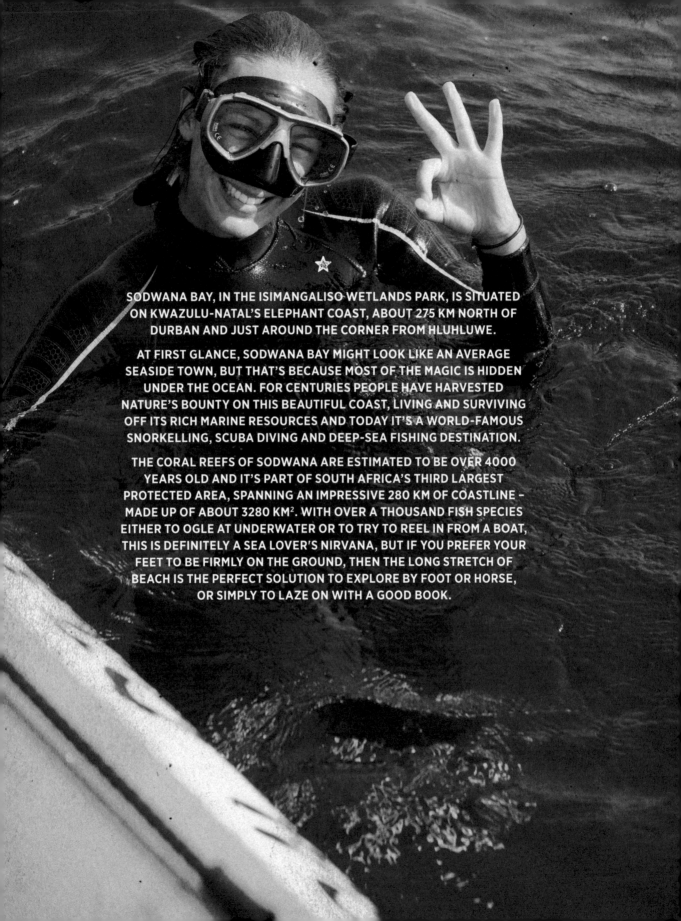

SODWANA BAY, IN THE ISIMANGALISO WETLANDS PARK, IS SITUATED ON KWAZULU-NATAL'S ELEPHANT COAST, ABOUT 275 KM NORTH OF DURBAN AND JUST AROUND THE CORNER FROM HLUHLUWE.

AT FIRST GLANCE, SODWANA BAY MIGHT LOOK LIKE AN AVERAGE SEASIDE TOWN, BUT THAT'S BECAUSE MOST OF THE MAGIC IS HIDDEN UNDER THE OCEAN. FOR CENTURIES PEOPLE HAVE HARVESTED NATURE'S BOUNTY ON THIS BEAUTIFUL COAST, LIVING AND SURVIVING OFF ITS RICH MARINE RESOURCES AND TODAY IT'S A WORLD-FAMOUS SNORKELLING, SCUBA DIVING AND DEEP-SEA FISHING DESTINATION.

THE CORAL REEFS OF SODWANA ARE ESTIMATED TO BE OVER 4000 YEARS OLD AND IT'S PART OF SOUTH AFRICA'S THIRD LARGEST PROTECTED AREA, SPANNING AN IMPRESSIVE 280 KM OF COASTLINE – MADE UP OF ABOUT 3280 KM^2. WITH OVER A THOUSAND FISH SPECIES EITHER TO OGLE AT UNDERWATER OR TO TRY TO REEL IN FROM A BOAT, THIS IS DEFINITELY A SEA LOVER'S NIRVANA, BUT IF YOU PREFER YOUR FEET TO BE FIRMLY ON THE GROUND, THEN THE LONG STRETCH OF BEACH IS THE PERFECT SOLUTION TO EXPLORE BY FOOT OR HORSE, OR SIMPLY TO LAZE ON WITH A GOOD BOOK.

★

THE TRICK TO REALLY TENDER CALAMARI OR SQUID IS TO BRAAI IT ON A HIGH HEAT, REALLY QUICKLY. IF IT COMES OUT TOUGH, DON'T BLAME ME. I WARNED YOU.

STUFFED CALAMARI TUBES

BY **MARTHINUS FERREIRA**

This will feed four not-so-hungry friends, and the stuffing is quite rich, so serve this as a light meal with good wine on a hot summer's night. First things first, get your hands on four fresh calamari tubes – double up if you have hungry friends or if the calamari tubes are quite small (keeping in mind that they shrink even more when cooked).

FOR THE STUFFING, YOU'LL NEED:

3 red, green and yellow peppers, one of each colour

a couple of pinches of paprika

1 tub of plain cream cheese

a couple of chillies, chopped – add more if you like it hot

juice of about half a lemon

a handful of basil, chopped

a handful of parsley, chopped

salt and cracked black pepper

★ THE STUFFING

Put the peppers on a grill over hot coals, turning them frequently until the skin is charred (pretty much blackened) right around. Take them off the heat and immediately pop into sandwich bags or something similar to sweat. After a couple of minutes you should be able to peel off the charred skin easily, leaving you only with the soft, sweet flesh of the peppers. Chop up the peppers, put them in a large mixing bowl and squash the flesh with a fork. Add to this the paprika, cream cheese, chopped chillies, lemon juice, basil and parsley, and season with salt and a couple of cracks of black pepper. Using the same fork, mix it together until everything is combined. Take about two to three tablespoons of the stuffing and scoop it into the calamari tubes. (Be careful not to overstuff the tubes – remember they shrink as they cook, so will burst if you overdo it.) Secure the open ends of each tube with a couple of toothpicks to prevent the stuffing from bursting out while you braai it. Carefully put the squid into a sandwich grid and set aside while you make the topping.

 ## ★ THE TOPPING

FOR THE TOPPING, YOU'LL NEED:
a big handful of baby brinjals
a glug of olive oil
a couple of garlic cloves, peeled and thinly sliced
salt and cracked black pepper, to taste
about 24 cherry tomatoes, on the vine
a small handful of basil, chopped
a small handful of parsley, chopped
a squeeze of lemon juice
a jar of caper berries

Timing is key here, because you need the calamari and the topping to be ready at the same time. This means you're going to have a couple of things sizzling on the braai simultaneously, so move around like Tom Cruise behind the bar in *Cocktail* (minus throwing bottles around and flirting with women ... depending on your skills).

First up, slice the baby brinjals in half – lengthways. Put a fireproof pan over moderate coals, add a glug of olive oil and once hot, add the brinjals and sliced garlic. Season with salt and pepper and fry until the brinjals are cooked and the garlic is golden brown. On the same fire, at about the same time, pop the vine tomatoes on the grid, face down, and right next to that, place the sandwiched calamari tubes. Now keep an eye on everything, making sure the veg doesn't burn and the calamari doesn't overcook or burst. (Told you, you need skills here!)

The calamari should be done after about two minutes a side. Take it off the heat and put it straight onto your serving plates. Remove the brinjals and garlic from the heat, and scoop the topping generously over the calamari. Arrange about six cherry tomatoes on each plate, then garnish with chopped basil and parsley. Finish it off with a drizzle of olive oil, a generous squeeze of fresh lemon juice, a couple of caper berries and a pinch of salt and cracked black pepper.

⭐

THOSE OF YOU WHO THINK CANNED TUNA IS DELICIOUS HAVE OBVIOUSLY NEVER EVER HAD FRESH LINE- OR POLE- CAUGHT YELLOWFIN TUNA! ONCE YOU'VE TASTED THE DIFFERENCE, CHANCES ARE THAT YOU'LL END UP GIVING THAT CAN OF 'TUNA' TO YOUR NEIGHBOUR'S CAT.

SEARED TUNA KEBABS

 ETIENNE & HEIN

YOU'LL NEED:

juice of 1 lemon

olive oil

a couple of pinches of smoked Maldon salt

a couple of pinches of cracked black pepper

a couple of pinches of chicken spice (yes, really)

a few pinches of paprika

1 fresh pole-caught yellowfin tuna loin, cut into cubes about 5 cm x 5 cm

1 pineapple, skin removed and cut into 2 cm-thick cubes

1 yellow pepper, cubed

Kikkoman soy sauce (optional)

⭐ TIPS

If you're using bamboo kebab sticks, soak them in water for about half an hour to prevent them from burning on the braai, or invest in a set of metal ones that you can re-use forever.

Two tips before you braai tuna: keep the flavours simple and don't overcook it – tuna is served best when it's still pink inside.

First up take a large mixing bowl and make a wet rub by mixing together lemon juice, olive oil and a couple of pinches each of smoked Maldon salt, cracked black pepper, chicken spice and paprika.

If you've already cubed the tuna and it looks all torn, you probably needed a sharper knife. If there's any leftover tuna, dip it into soy sauce and enjoy immediately. Now, take the cubes of tuna, put them into the mixing bowl and rub the lemon and spices into and onto the flesh. Let it rest for 20 minutes or longer.

In the meantime, add a dash of oil to a fireproof pan and fry the pineapple with a pinch of paprika until the pineapple starts caramelising. Remove from the heat, allow to cool and then start putting it all together. Skewer a cube of tuna, a slice of pineapple and a pepper onto a kebab stick and repeat – but be careful not to overcrowd the kebab. Heat a fireproof pan over moderate coals and sear the tuna kebabs on each side (about two minutes a side). You can also skip the pan-frying and just do it straight on a braai grid.

 Extra lemon wedges and good wine.

BERTUS IS A GENIUS WHEN IT COMES TO MAKING REALLY SIMPLE BUT FRESH AND DELICIOUS FOOD. NOTHING FANCY ON THE ROAD – JUST REAL FOOD THAT WILL MAKE YOU SMILE FROM DEEP WITHIN YOUR WANNABE-FOODIE SOUL. THE LIST OF WHAT YOU CAN DO WITH RICE IS ENDLESS: RICE WITH GRAVY, RISOTTO, STIR-FRIED RICE ... BUT IF YOU EVER HAVE CHICKEN OR PRAWNS ON THE BRAAI, THIS IS THE WAY TO GO.

COCONUT FRIED RICE

 BERTUS BASSON

YOU'LL NEED:

30 g white sugar

300 g jasmine rice, cooked

½ tin of coconut milk

100 g mung bean sprouts

50 g spring onion, sliced

50 ml fish sauce

50 g coconut shavings, toasted

10 g fresh coriander

juice of 1 lime

Put a wok straight on the open coals of a medium to hot fire. Add the sugar, stir continuously until it's melted and caramelised, then add the rice and keep stirring. Once the rice starts to get darker, add the coconut milk and fry for a few minutes. Then add the bean sprouts, spring onion and fish sauce. Take it off the heat and garnish with the coconut shavings, coriander and a generous squeeze of lime.

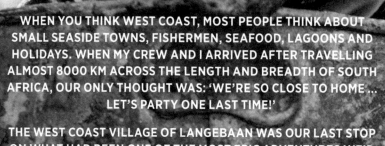

WHEN YOU THINK WEST COAST, MOST PEOPLE THINK ABOUT SMALL SEASIDE TOWNS, FISHERMEN, SEAFOOD, LAGOONS AND HOLIDAYS. WHEN MY CREW AND I ARRIVED AFTER TRAVELLING ALMOST 8000 KM ACROSS THE LENGTH AND BREADTH OF SOUTH AFRICA, OUR ONLY THOUGHT WAS: 'WE'RE SO CLOSE TO HOME … LET'S PARTY ONE LAST TIME!'

THE WEST COAST VILLAGE OF LANGEBAAN WAS OUR LAST STOP ON WHAT HAD BEEN ONE OF THE MOST EPIC ADVENTURES WE'D EVER BEEN ON, AND IT WAS TIME TO CELEBRATE THAT. AND WHAT BETTER WAY THAN TO LIGHT OUR FIRES ONE LAST TIME AND HAVE THE ULTIMATE BRING AND BRAAI?

SA'S FAVOURITE PASTIME

It happens, all over the country every single weekend. It's as sure as eggs are eggs. It's inevitable. It's part of the blueprint of our country. It happens, no matter what type of weather, because our weekends would be weird without it. It's the build-up before the big match or the aftermath of a great party. It's an excuse to be outside. To see our friends. To crack open a cold one before lunch. It's our reason for lighting a fire. It's a national obsession. It's our identity.

We've been doing it for decades, but WOW do we get it wrong sometimes. The burnt steak. The warm beer. The no beer. The latecomers. The guy who arrives with frozen chicken. The verlepte slaai. The strange oke who takes his jokes that one joke too far. The awkward silence that follows. The potjie that tastes like mushy stew. The bad music. The pile of dishes that keep on coming.

But sometimes we get it juuuust right. The perfect steak. The heap of ice-cold beer, waiting on ice in the bathtub. The just-on-timers. The crunchy fresh salad. The potjie that is layered perfectly and whispers to you while you wait. The good music. The friend who helps you wash (and even dry and pack away) the pile of dirty dishes.

It's the BRING and BRAAI.

And that is what a braai,
a "kuier" is all about.
Nothing can beat it.

THE BEGINNER'S GUIDE TO BECOMING A BRAAI MASTER

TYPES OF WOOD

When you choose the type of wood you're going to braai with, stick to the local stuff.

Black Wattle: Great for building that bonfire on the beach or when you're camping.

Rooikrans: My favourite go-to braai wood.

Vine stumps: Make kiff coals – fast.

Kameeldoring: From dead trees only, please! Makes very hot coals and because it's so dense, it sometimes burns straight through the night.

Compressed charcoal: Ain't no friend of mine.

Real charcoal: With you all the way.

Pine wood: Don't even think about it, unless you like an unpleasant resin-flavoured steak.

★

BUILDING THE BEST FIRE

This is a debate that's bound to happen at many braais and not getting the fire right is enough to make even the biggest burly man's hand shake. Some of us pack the wood like you would imagine building a log cabin, but the trick here is to fill the gaps with kindling. Other people (lazy people) just throw an entire bag of charcoal on top of loads of firelighters. Whichever way you do it (and I sincerely hope it's not the lazy-people way), I can only give you one piece of advice. When your fire is burning, leave it alone to burn down to those perfect hot coals you need.

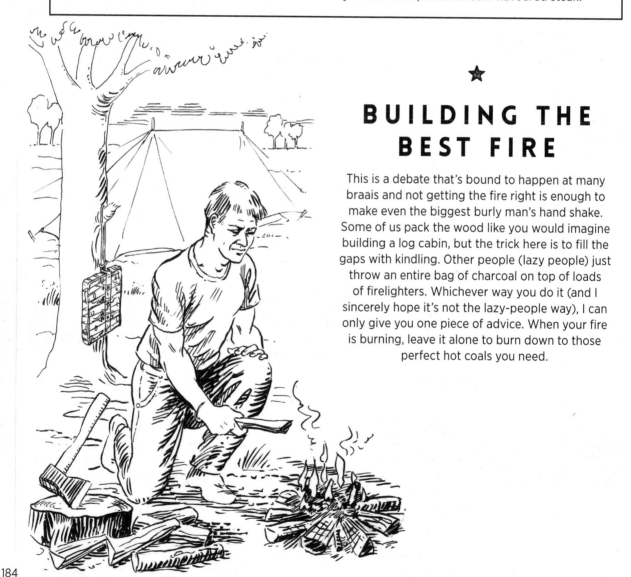

THE BEGINNER'S GUIDE TO BECOMING A BRAAI MASTER

COAL TEMPERATURE

Sitting around waiting for someone to start braaiing already can be tedious. Especially if you're hungry. Especially if you know that the really nice salad you made is getting warm and verlep and that you'll have to reheat the garlic bread ... again. But if you know the temperatures of the coals, you'll be able to serve everything hot off the coals with all the sides done spot on time for the ultimate braai.

THIS IS WHAT YOU DO.

Hold your hand about 10 cm above the braai. Then count slowly. The moment your hand starts burning (not cooking!), remove it and remember to where you counted.

TWO TO THREE SECONDS ### HOT COALS *Perfect for steaks and chops.*	**THREE TO FOUR SECONDS** ### MODERATE TO HOT COALS *Perfect for certain chicken pieces and fish, and great to finish off steaks and chops.*
FIVE TO EIGHT SECONDS ### MODERATE COALS *Good for boerewors and other chicken and fish dishes, baking bread, simmering potjies and cooking puddings.*	**NINE OR MORE SECONDS** ### ADD MORE WOOD *Your fire is probably almost dead, so add more wood!*

THE PERFECT STEAK

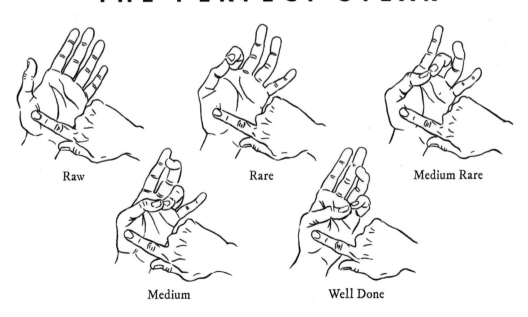

Raw

Rare

Medium Rare

Medium

Well Done

THE BEGINNER'S GUIDE TO BECOMING A BRAAI MASTER

POTJIE

A little TLC goes a long way ... If you're lucky enough to have just bought yourself a new potjie, you should know how to take care of it. If you do it right, your kids will be lucky enough to inherit it from you one day ...

Scrub the inside of the pot with sandpaper, then wash it out with warm soapy water and grease the inside of the pot with oil. Place over a hot fire and once the pot and oil is hot, wipe it clean with a paper towel or that T-shirt your wife's been threatening to throw out. Be careful not to burn yourself. Once you see what's on that paper towel, you'll be very (VERY) happy that you've gone to the trouble. Now repeat the process, wiping clean with a new paper towel or the side of the T-shirt that you haven't used yet. Keep doing this until it comes out clean.

To prevent the potjie from rusting you need to give it a loving bath after every potjie meal you cook. Do this by simply washing it out with warm soapy water, then drying it and rubbing a bit of vegetable oil on the insides, scrunching up your morning paper and placing it inside. Store it away in a cool, dry place.

THE NUMBER GAME

For those of you who didn't know this, potjie pots come in numbers, and these numbers are actually different sizes, and these different sizes will tell you how many people you can feed. So before you go and buy a new potjie, know which number to get.

No. 1	Feeds four.
No. 2	Feeds eight.
No. 3	Feeds 12.
No. 4	Feeds 16.
No. 6	Feeds 22.
No. 8	Feeds 30.
No. 10	Feeds 46.
No. 14	Feeds 58.
No. 20	Feeds 94.
No. 25	Go ahead, have a party!

THE BEGINNER'S GUIDE TO BECOMING A BRAAI MASTER

BRING A CAST-IRON PAN BACK TO LIFE

So, you've got a non-stick cast-iron pan, but even the best ones never last a lifetime. I use the crêpe pan my grandmother gave me when I was a lightie. And it still works. The secret? I salt it before I use it. So, before you give up on your old faithful pan, try this nifty trick. First up, put the pan on a high heat, and get it smoking hot, then pour in loads of fine sea salt (enough to cover the base). Let the salt sit and turn dark brown, then toss the browned salt in the dustbin and wipe off any salt still stuck to the base of the pan. Add a splash of oil into the pan and wipe it into the surface of the pan. You've just created a non-stick pan!

BEST DOUGH

Whenever you're making dough or pastry from scratch, there are a couple of very important tricks to remember. The first? For dough, ingredients must be at room temperature. For pastry? Keep it cold: cold hands, cold butter, cold liquid … you get the picture. The second? Proof the dough. You do this to relax the gluten (the protein in flour which gives dough its elasticity) and to let the yeast do it's job – that is, letting it be the driving force in fermentation, allowing the dough to double in size. And the last important trick? To lightly grease and cover the dough while it's proofing – this way you prevent the dough from drying out. That's why even when you activate yeast, you sprinkle a bit of flour over the top of the yeast to stop it from drying out and forming a crust.

RESTING MEAT

If you're really hungry, this is the worst part of any braai, but if you have the patience to wait just that little longer, it's going to make a world of difference. Let me explain: When meat cooks, the muscle fibres push out moisture and firm up, so when you take the meat off the braai, the lost moisture will be reabsorbed into the meat. If you don't wait for at least 5 minutes before cutting the meat, all those lovely juices will pour out and you'll end up with a very dry steak or roast. So, the lesson? Just be patient!

THANK YOU!

This is both the best and the worst part of any book I write. The best part, because I get a chance to thank everyone involved in making the show and the book such a success – from colleagues to friends and family. And the worst part, because I always end up forgetting to thank someone, which inevitably leads to me being k*kked on when I see the said forgotten person.

But here goes, and if I somehow left out your name (you'll know who you are when you read this), please know that I am eternally and sincerely grateful to you anyway.

To all the teams who competed in *Ultimate Braai Master II: The Roads Less Travelled*, and for sharing your recipes with me. Thank you to: Nicole Buirman, Suzanne Nel, Collin du Plessis, Matt Bronkhorst, Kate George, Jonno Proudfoot, Thabiso Motloung, Motebejane Mofokeng, Jacques Bester, Nadia Botha, Kyle Hodgson, Rudy Gibbons, Martin Sebelebele, Ziza Masemola, Ashok Naidoo, Jolene Arries, Quenten Alberts, Sandy Alberts, Chris Kastern, Simon Good, Andrew Leeuw, Nomthandazo Sithole, Nonkululeko Zondo, Lebo Thebe, Tomas Cunnama, Daniel Cunnama, Etienne Gersbach, Hein Gersbach, Shaun Cavanagh, Samantha Van Niekerk.

Thank you to my wife Eugenie for allowing me to follow my dreams and for chasing them with me. Then of course, as always, my mom Jeanne, sons Dan and Samuel, my dad Carlos and sister Tanya and her family.

Then to my incredible *Cooked* family for sticking it out and burning the midnight oil: Peter Gird, Roshni Haraldsen, Sunel Haasbroek, Wesley Volschenk, Raylene Stevens, Megan Bryan, Lara Black, Jei Lindeque, Kirsty Abbey, Mishal Fortune, Rugayah Essop, Herman Wärnich, Stephen Kramer, Grant Poole, Robert Whitehead, Brian Waters, Charl Cater, Zahir Isaacs, Darren Ilett, Brad Theron, Ian Belknap, Llewellyn Rice, Tasneem Ozman, Georgie Caldow, Matthew Abraham, Megan Rainier, JanieB Smit and Lutfiy-yah Blooms. The thanks offered here cannot adequately express my gratitude to all of you.

Once again, Bertus Basson and Marthinus Ferreira – you have become lifelong friends and I can't wait to go on a new adventure next year!

Then, in no particular order, a huge shout out to: Megan Tinkler, Andrew Faber, John Bennett, Luke Retief, Sakura Butler, Simon Joyner, John Ebako, Mike Nyembe, Travis Nel, Josh Yon, Bradley Vincent, Niel de Villiers, Wula Veldskoen, Leon Liebenberg, Danny Kodesh, Kai Auchincloss (your crew portraits rock!), Christo Myburgh, Shaun Harrison, Nicola Austin, Luke Longmore, Johann Joubert, Warren Cupido, Joe Dawson, Greg Chater, Leighla McGregor, Zola Mdladla, Peace Chari, Cyril Anyanga, Vuyo Nyamza (for the endless cups of coffee and toasted sarmies), Lervano Solomons, Lorraine Hirst, Sphamandla Kaboka, Basil Smith, Gareth Beaumont, Grant Spooner and the team at Tenacity! Let's do it all over again soon!

Thanks to the talented Penguin team: Kelly Norwood-Young, Genevieve Adams, Janet Bartlet, Frederik de Jager and Ellen van Schalkwyk. Another book, done and dusted!

To Quinton Bruton and Toby Attwell – you guys never cease to excite and surprise me. Thanks for pushing the boundaries and designing yet another book that is nothing less than incredible. Twoshoes for president!!!

To Janet Gird, my fearless recipe tester – thank you for all your research and hours of testing recipes and using your family as guinea pigs! Thank goodness the boys and Girdy are still alive.

To my brilliant photographers Louis Hiemstra and Dominique Little: from strength to strength we go. How do I say thank you for capturing the reality of the journey so beautifully and keeping the memories alive via the lens?

Thanks to Caro Gardner, food stylist extraordinaire: I don't know how you do it. Making this cook's humble offerings look so appealing – you are a brilliant and welcome friend to my oddball family.

To my writer, Helena Lombard – how you get in my head, make sense of the garbled voice memos and manage to hold this slippery eel down – is beyond me. Thank you so, so much for having the patience to hit the road with me, for meeting deadlines, for holding it together, for being the consummate professional.

Then last, but not least, special thanks to our sponsors and partners: Pick n Pay (Malcolm Mycroft, Yvonne Short), Coca-Cola (Jodie Bailey-Norris, Marina Caldow, Ramokone Ledwaba), Standard Bank, Renault SA (Fabien Payzan, Lee-Anne Stanton), BIC (Bridgette Mandava), Front Runner (Renee Cary), Drostdy-Hof (Louis van Brakel), Kikkoman, Consol, Cadac, and all our generous location hosts, including the Farmhouse Hotel in Langebaan, who provided us with a home-from-home along this epic journey, proving that hospitality is as much a part of the South African landscape as its beautiful vistas and wide open spaces!

Here's to our next fireside adventure!

INDEX

INDEX